49

VOLUME 01

Isabelle Bisson-Routhier

*This book is dedicated to my best friend, Grace.
Her kindness and support are unmatched, and I
adore her with all that I am, both for her soul and
the help she has given me.*

I hope to one day repay this kindness tenfold.

A FEATHER IN THE BREEZE

AVELINE WISHWOOD

The end began on a misty day.

A day of hazy light and ivory skies, like the days and the months and the eons before. A day spent in a high, spiralling palace, made of crystalline bricks and thick, engraved glass, balanced amongst treetops and bird-nests and clouds.

A day where Aveline was trapped, guarded, protected.

But not for much longer.

Aveline's footsteps were light, though her borrowed boots were sturdy. A feathered cloak concealed her wings, blessed with an illusion that would encourage eyes to slide away. A dozen books were tucked into her bag, stuffed with fairy-tales and fluff. The weight slowed her down.

She dodged a pair of maids, twittering like birds as they carried stacks of folded sheets. Her head ducked as she hurried past a gathering of guards, their beaked masks reflecting her half-hidden face. And she darted through every hallway as swiftly as she could, aiming not to be spotted at all.

A faint illusion could only do so much, especially when worn by someone of an entirely different magic, but it was all she had. And she had to get out of there.

Aveline picked up the pace.

It would not take long for the rest of the palace to discover she was missing. Rumours would spread like wildfire: flashes of heat amongst an otherwise ever-icy kingdom. Their lives were boring, after all.

The war had yet to burrow into the heart of her kingdom of Awin. It lingered on the borders to the sea; it raged on in their tiny island colonies; it had lasted for generations. A natural hatred between her people of Air and their people of Storms, a war born from ancient gods.

But Aveline knew little more on the subject than that. Who would tell an innocent princess such things, after all?

Her lips pressed together as she ducked behind a thick bookcase, waiting for the flock of advisors to move on. They passed her with words like bitter birdsongs and did not cast her a glance.

Aveline continued.

She stepped over the scattered toys of servant children, cast glances through unfamiliar doorways, and only slowed a little when the sweet singing of her human sister reached her ears. Elodie was two towers away, at least, but the breeze had always cherished her song.

Aveline pushed the thought aside, dodging a

gaggle of goose-pets, waddling the hallways like they owned the place. It almost made her smile, but she pushed away her fondness, too.

Most doors to the palace were heavily guarded, as cages were wont to be. And though the window-walls allowed sun-streaked clouds and watercolour mist to drift through, it was far more of a challenge for an almost-human to slip through: even for followers of the goddess of Air.

Aveline gritted her teeth, turned a corner, and further quickened her pace, darting to the rhythm of her heartbeat.

There was one splintered door she wished to reach, tucked between a statue and a painting, leading to a path of braided tree-limbs: unsteady, but speckled with flowers. Abandoned. Aveline may not have known what lay beyond it, but she was readier than ever to explore.

She would not flee for long, but it would be long enough.

Aveline reached for a knotted door-knob, leading to an unexplored hallway. Her fingers curled around it, but it flew open first, whacking her in the face. With a yelp, she fell onto her backside, hand flying to the sting on her cheek.

Her eyes rose to meet the gaze above her. Masked.

A guard.

Aveline could hardly breathe. And that only worsened upon the realisation that her hood had slipped, exposing her flushed face and grey eyes and loose hair like strands of white mist.

Shit.

Aveline ignored the outstretching hand. She leapt to her feet, shoving past with an elbow to their ribcage. It knocked into solid metal, pain spiking in her arm, but she paid no heed to her panic-born stupidity.

The guard called after her, and Aveline bit her tongue in her efforts not to curse aloud. As she turned a corner, she unclasped her cloak, allowing it to flutter to the floorboards like a feather.

Aveline unfurled her wings, barely rising above the floor as a metal hand reached to snatch her. She soared to the ceiling, pressing hands to the glass and breathing the sweet mistberry scent that filled much of her kingdom, seeping through every crack in the windows and walls.

The glass was too sturdy to shatter, though that was not something to be considered. What if the fractured rain hurt an innocent? Her temporary escape was not worth such a thing.

Aveline took a breath, and her head snapped to look left, right, down. Guards gathered below, calling to the princess they were not meant to command. It would not take long before those with their own magics of Air would rise and join her.

And then where would she go?

Aveline cursed behind painted palms and marble teeth, casting her eyes back and forth once again. Her gaze flicked over puffs of mist, curling murals, and thick bookshelves that reached from floor-to-ceiling and wall-to-wall. The only ways out were on the ground.

She bit her tongue and drew blood, painting copper across her pale lips. And then, she stopped.

Her wings no longer flapped to the beating of her heart.

And she fell.

Down. Down. Down.

Aveline landed silently, crouching, and then stood and surged forward, passing the door she had once wished to enter. The maze of her palace bemused even her, but she would find *somewhere* to break free, even if not the original door.

She swallowed her terror, ducking under a statue and dodging the shining swords and hands that chased her. They were not quite quick enough, but her energy would not last for long.

Her heartbeat overwhelmed her panting breaths.

She could do this.

Aveline turned a corner, and her bag's fabric snagged on the blade of a suit of armour, tearing a hole big enough that books wept through and trailed behind her. She did not slow, though curses slipped through her lips. Inaudible to all not her.

A rope of Air wrapped around her throat – invisible, intangible, but *real* – and Aveline choked, yanked back by it. She landed on a fallen book, digging into her hip and making her groan.

Her eyelids fluttered, before the magic released

her, allowing her to breathe freely once again. She panted like it had been years.

Aveline's head snapped to the one who had caught her, and she locked gazes with the wolf-grey eyes of her mother. Narrow and cold. Her white locks were tightly fashioned into an elaborate crown. Her hand was balled into a fist, gripping her magic as firmly as possible.

For a second, Aveline believed she would be struck. Instead, however, Queen Aladie snapped her fingers. A pair of guards grabbed Aveline by the arms, yanking her to her feet.

"Aveline?"

Aveline swallowed. "Yes, mother?"

"There are certain privileges granted to those who are heir to the throne. You are ever-donned in riches. You feast upon delicacies at every opportunity. Your kingdom worships you."

Her kingdom hardly knew her.

"You have the knowledge that is withheld from peasants."

An insulting lie.

"You have your every wish granted."

Even falser.

"You have boundless power at your fingertips."

Before she could stop herself, Aveline snorted.

She did not have the time to smother the treacherous sound. She did not have the time to immediately apologise. But her mother certainly had the time to strike her across the face, hard enough that, had Aveline not been held up by two guards, she would have fallen.

Aveline gritted her teeth, and did not meet her mother's gaze, not even as it bore into her soul. She kept her breaths even, kept herself as still as could be, until she realised she was supposed to respond.

She rose her head. "I was not fleeing forever," she murmured. "I simply wanted time to myself. Time to explore. Time to learn."

Freedom.

Aladie's fingers brushed her daughter's blooming bruise. She sighed as if this was nothing but tiresome. "If you wish to learn, then you shall be taken to a place of learning." She turned on her heel. "You two, fetch a potion of healing. The rest of you, ensure she follows me *closely.*"

Aveline swallowed a sigh.

Aladie scoffed as if she could hear her daughter's every thought – and what a terror would that be? "The one thing princesses like yourself shall never have, Aveline, is freedom. You should know that by now."

A shiver danced down Aveline's spine.

She may not have freedom now, she supposed.

But, as queen, she would be able to change that.

She would be able to change *everything.*

❀ ❀ ❀

Silent.

Aveline was meant to grit her teeth. Aveline was meant to swallow her tongue. Aveline was meant to be silent.

A cloud, streaked with an iridescent glow – like a watercolour painting dipped in mist – was all there was to hold her gaze.

It slipped through the tower's glass walls, shimmering and sparkling like her favourite light-and-feather gown, reserved only for the most elegant of balls. She could picture such events with a wistful clarity: the days-long dances upon thick canopies of limbs and leaves; the treetops spanning miles in every direction; the luminous birds that twittered and fluttered, keeping the night from bathing her in shadow.

All were so high above the ground that the earth was but a distant memory. Forgotten.

Perhaps those not of the Air would have feared living in palaces and villages so high in the trees, amongst bronze branches and cerulean blue, shrouded in sun-streaked mist. Invisible to the wasteland of stumps and roots and corpses below.

It would have been so easy to fall. It *was* easy to fall.

But it was all she, and her people of Awin, had ever known.

"Aveline?" came that cold, familiar voice.

Her eyes snapped from the cloud – already fading from her fickle memory – and to those who gathered around the large, crystal table she was not permitted to be so close to, though her presence in this meeting was a requirement. A punishment. A mockery.

Aveline could watch from across the room. She could listen to the words she hardly understood. But the maps and plans, laid out with ink and spider silk, were not yet hers to witness.

There were only sixteen with such power.

The fourteen most important Awinian advisors and aristocrats, and Aveline's parents. King Barke Wishwood. Queen Aladie Wishwood.

The queen held all the power of Awin in the bejewelled palms of her hands. And yet her daughters could only know the barest of bones: even the one meant to inherit that power.

Aveline's lips downturned, then smoothed over. She straightened in her cushioned seat, folding one pale hand over the other and crossing her right ankle over her left. Her thighs stung, but the pink scratches, etched by her own polished nails, would fade. And no one but servants sworn to secrecy had ever known of her little, subtle rebellion.

"Yes, mother?"

All eyes were now on her.

Aveline ensured her wings were neatly folded against her back, her feathers as white as crystal clouds, though lacking the iridescence. Her hair, of a similar shade, was now pinned in an elaborate braid: a crown around her head, dotted with suns, clouds, and moons.

She was almost more jewellery than girl.

Aladie watched her daughter: narrow-eyed and prim. "Have you considered any of the suitors we have presented to you?"

Aveline's hands twitched into claws. She almost repeated the question in a mocking tone. But she was no fool. She smoothed her knuckles without casting them a glance, eyes flitting all around the room, watching all who watched.

"Aveline?"

"None would be right to share a throne with, mother."

Aladie raised an eyebrow. "Are those your only qualms with your duties, Aveline? You may not like your lover-to-be, no matter how right for the throne they could become. Your personal taste is irrelevant."

"I understand," Aveline said: mimicking the tone. "I care only for the future of our kingdom, and that is all I am taking into consideration."

"If you are not married quickly, you could be stolen."

"I know, mother."

"We wish not for you to be eternally wed to an enemy."

"I know, mother."

Aladie pursed her lips.

Aveline could hardly breathe, could hardly *move,* until the rhythm of the meeting resumed: a song she had always so despised. Her shoulders slumped, before again straightening.

For a few minutes, Aveline tried to listen, tried to understand, but they cared not for what she had been asked, as if it mattered even less than she did.

Instead, they discussed their fleets of sea-ships and sky-ships, and where to position them in case of an attack.

Aveline found her mind drifting.

She scanned the octagonal room, with a guard stationed at every corner: between the thick panes of glass that made up the majority of the walls. There were two men on either side of the white-and-grey doors, the tips of their swords on the floor between their boots.

They were dressed in light metal, with the beaked masks of a bird she did not recognise. Her father – in his days before silence – had always insisted they were modelled after reality, but Aveline spent much of her time with palms pressed against windows. She had never seen a bird with such wide eyes and curved feathers.

And she had never seen a bird with fingers that twitched and wriggled like snakes, even while wrapped in thick metal gloves: almost crescent moons. Twinkling in the sunlight.

No bird had darkness dancing amongst fingertips, either.

Streaked with moonlight. Speckled with stars.

No one else had noticed the dancing magic of a knight who looked just like the rest: when masked, at least. No one else had noticed the way he made Aveline's heart beat like a hummingbird's wings.

Her stomach's swirls grew nauseating, like a hurricane of twigs scraping her belly from the inside out.

Aveline looked away from Adonis, who she was certain was watching *her* – eyes hidden behind the littlest slits of his beaked mask – and returned her focus to the meeting she so despised.

If she had been included, if they had not spoken with maps and plans she could not see, perhaps she would not have loathed them so deeply.

Perhaps. Perhaps not.

Speech-snippets bubbled to the surface of understanding.

"Styrmish ships have now thrice been spotted at our northern sea," hissed a hunched, elderly man, a dragonfly tail protruding from a hole in his robes. "Considering their position at our south, it seems they wish to be *subtle* in their investigations. They may be sending spies, assassins, soldiers. Followers to hunt and destroy us!"

His fist slammed against the table, hard enough that Aveline half-expected it to shatter, or at the very least crack. It did not flinch, nor did those gathered around him: far too used to this advisor's spiels of hatred and fury. Passion was charming, in an odd sort of way.

"They wish to overtake our colonies of the sky."

"They wish to steal back what is not theirs to rescind."

"Their magic is the *antithesis* to ours, to everything we stand for. Air and Storms. Awin and Styrme. We have been enemies since the age of the gods. They wish to destroy us, to take all we have built!"

The elderly advisor hissed like a serpentine beetle. "We should return this intrusion in kind," he spat. Mist gathered around his torso, painting greyish smears across his skin. "We—"

Aladie raised a silent hand and his next words died on his tongue.

"War is not what Awin needs," she said, speaking as if to an audience of grandeur. "An alliance is our only solution."

An alliance with Arelc and Alyro.

The three kingdoms of the Air – nestled together to make one island – would be far stronger united, fearsome enough to frighten any foe, even those with the powers of Styrme. Their armies would be a force unmatched. And, even without a strengthened bond, those of the Air already held a privilege that most followers did not: more than one kingdom following a single magic, a single *goddess.*

An alliance was far from an impossibility.

The last three centuries had soothed their relations, even as Awin and Alyro had once been at odds. Though tension often lingered like soft, billowing smoke, the trio now traded with open arms.

But an alliance was better strengthened with two souls bound, hearts never parting. A spell that every kingdom partook in, and most never allowed undoing, even through death. Marriage was little more than entrapment. And yet, the crown princess needed a spouse.

A spouse of *importance*, no less.

If only Aveline could wed an enemy, she often thought in a bitter, rebellious tone. That would end a war like nothing else could, and perhaps it would grant her the freedom she had always so desired. But that was not her mother's intention.

She knew the kinds of people her parents wished to gift her to.

Aveline ducked her head, her pinned hair refusing to slip out of place, and looked to the floor beneath her now-bare feet, her whitish skin decorated with blurs of snowbells and ivy.

The floorboards were propped up by branches, speckled with flowers in every shape and hue. Aveline's toe brushed a blossom in similar shades of petal and pearl as her dress: loose, delicate, and decorated with plumage and diamonds. She almost wished to tear it to shreds.

Would this flower's honey-sun pollen and mist-speckled petals make a fitting decoration for her hair? She could slip it behind her ear, some colour against her ivory locks. Aveline began to reach to pluck it, already picturing thorns between the flesh of her fingertips.

But the words she had tuned out ceased, and the clearing of a throat caught her attention.

Aveline's spine straightened as if she had committed some heinous crime, but when her eyes locked with her mother's, she found no disapproval. Instead, her gaze remained cool, unbothered, unreadable. But that was to be expected.

They remained locked together for several moments, before Aladie's lips parted once more. "Aveline," she said. "You may go."

Aveline stood, fingers curling.

She would give almost anything for a blade to be placed into her palm, or even a suitably-sharp shard of glass.

Her hands unfurled, sliding over her delicate dress. Her fingers caught on white jewels, though did not quite tug them loose. She fell into as deep a bow as she could stomach.

All but Aladie and Barke returned the gesture, and a few mumbled gentle farewells to the princess said to be beloved by her people.

"Of course, mother. May I take my guardian with me?"

"You may."

Aveline breathed a sigh of relief.

She nodded, turning to Adonis, whose swirling darkness slipped away as if folding into a crease in the air. He crossed the room with quick, careful steps, accompanied by the melodious clanking of light armour, and passed the table he knew better than to glance at. He reached for the doors, opening the left in one swift motion – no small feat – and gestured grandly for Aveline to come through.

She rolled her eyes at his dramatics, but made no comment. As she tiptoed across the room, he allowed her to pass him, and then followed wordlessly as she descended a staircase of cool, curling wood.

As they reached its foot, they crossed a long hallway – past guards who did not twitch, maids who curtseyed until they were out of sight, and warbling birds the colours of honey and milk – until, finally, they found themselves alone.

She stopped, and he stopped beside her.

Adonis began to laugh, as if that were all that resided in his belly. He removed his mask, tossing it into the air, catching it, before hanging it on his belt with a ragged cream ribbon.

His curls were the same midnight as his magic of the Dark, and his black-and-white eyes were speckled night skies, filled with that which the gods did not permit them to know. Stars, shimmering like diamonds, were scattered across his deep brown skin, the only visible cluster being the dozen that climbed his neck like ivy on a wall.

Aveline's eyes lingered.

"I heard you had quite the adventure." Adonis grinned down at her, prompting her whole body to flush pink. "You must not have been missing for long, though. I only heard the rumours afterwards."

Aveline huffed. "It was hardly an adventure. I was looking for a place to read alone, perhaps a place to stroll."

"A place to uncover secrets, you mean."

"Am I not permitted to have multiple aspirations?"

Adonis laughed again. "You are the princess, if I remember correctly: granted one aspiration for the length of your existence."

"And you are my guard, if *I* remember correctly. You are supposed to remain at my side or at my door without pause. How did you get away with that abandonment, Adonis?"

"I traded posts for an hour."

"Why is that?"

Adonis flashed his pearl-white teeth. "Must you know all, your highness? Aren't you used to secrets by now?"

Aveline glared, but even she could not hold onto venom for long. A sigh overtook her, heavy and trembling. Her fingers furled into fists, before unfurling and laying limp at her sides.

The weight of Adonis's gaze was palpable.

"I must say," he cut through the silence, his voice as rich, smooth, and sweet as rising dawn. "I didn't understand a word they discussed in there, though that may have been the point."

Aveline's sigh swirled with whistles of wind. "Then I suppose you're as knowledgeable as I am. They wish to hide their secrets from their guards with coded words, and I am just as likely to learn nothing at all."

What would it take for true knowledge, true freedom?

Adonis placed a hand on Aveline's shoulder. Its imagined heat seeped through her sleeve, warming her blood like an ever-lit flame, though his metal gloves remained a barrier unbreakable.

He squeezed, eyes twinkling. "I suspect you know *something*. You are our princess, after all."

Aveline looked away, though made no effort to remove his hand.

With all his secrets, she would not have been surprised if he knew the troubles of her kingdom better than she did. But Aveline had learned long ago that Adonis knew how to stay silent, and it helped more than it hindered her. For him, she allowed it.

Adonis's thumb traced a circle on her sleeve, delicate enough that even her easily-bruised skin simply yearned for more. She often yearned for that which she could not have.

Aveline almost began to chuckle, too, though hers would have been far more bitter. An unwelcome taste on her sugar-coated tongue. She did not allow the laughter to do anything more than linger in the back of her throat, nor did she allow it to choke her.

"I'll know when I take the throne. They will allow me that, at least. That, and nothing more." Her brow furrowed, lips twisting into an unhidden scowl. "I am sick of secrets, but what else is there to do? I beg and I flee and I listen, but I hear nothing at all!"

Aveline was only as knowledgeable as her parents allowed her to be.

Her eyes flicked back to Adonis, finding something strange in the depths of his gaze. After a moment, he shook away whatever thought had plagued him. "Not all secrets shall be kept from you forever."

She raised an eyebrow. "Are yours included?"

His lips twitched. "Perhaps."

Aveline rolled her eyes. "And how long shall it be until everything is spilled? Will I only hear the secrets of Awin on my deathbed?"

"You won't." Adonis cracked a musing smile. "But you may have years until then, I'm afraid. Your parents are in good health. There is, it would seem, plenty more time to do as they wish, before the kingdom follows you above all but our gods. Like I do."

Aveline raised an eyebrow. "Do you?"

"I try."

"You take joy in bothering me."

"Ha! Well, you've got me there, swan."

"Everyone else says my feathers are of doves."

Adonis chuckled. "Everyone else is mistaken."

In reality, Aveline's wings were neither one nor the other. Her feathers were white and soft, resistant against the wind and rain that often came, though she was seldom below the clouds. They were not quite the right shape for either bird. They were, like the masks her knights wore, adjacent to reality, but imperfect imitations.

But her people – above, below, or alongside her status – liked to define things as one or the other. They were not quite so filled with daydreams as those of Arelc, nor so wild and unpredictable as the people of Alyro.

Doves seemed fitting for a princess known for her gentle temperament. Swans had too much bite.

"I know you better than everyone else, *swan*." Adonis leant in, another smile pulling at his dark lips. His voice lowered, just a little, though there was not a soul to overhear. "Don't you trust me?"

Aveline's eyes flicked to the floor. Did she?

A moment passed. Two. Three.

"Perhaps."

She paused, listening to nothing but the wind and his breaths, before she tentatively met his eyes once more, finding them having never left her behind. They seldom did, it seemed.

He captured her gaze for far longer than any princess and knight had need for, and yet she could not escape. But even as her eyes remained locked with his, her heart remained locked away, too. Aveline's ribs made for an unbreakable cage.

She could not give what she could not set free.

Adonis stepped back, breaking the trance and taking his touch along with him. He lowered onto one knee, amplifying her heartbeat, and his metal-wrapped hand made its way into her right. He lifted it to his lips, and pressed a kiss to the knuckle that sent shivers down her spine.

She knew what she yearned for, what filled her belly and bones with warmth and desire. And he knew what she wanted, too.

They both knew what they could not have.

Adonis's irises sparkled like a starry night,

holding much that she wished to explore. "The only freedom I can grant you is this. Shall we visit your pond?" His lips curled, his eyes focused and dark – shadowed under his brow and whispering a longing that could never truly be reciprocated – though his words kept a merry lilt. "We may even find a suitor you and your parents will *both* love along the way."

Aveline's face flushed, and she cast a glance at the wall beside them: ivory-white, and covered with murals of Awin's past and future rulers – who had reigned for the centuries behind them, and who they believed would reign in eternities to come. The final remained only silhouettes.

She could not ignore the golden-winged mural that only looked a little like herself. Its outline did not blur, not even when she peered through misty eyes.

"Perhaps," she said, though she suspected she had been silent for longer than was ordinary, filling the air with nothing but breaths. "I have no duties for two more hours, so I might as well find something to entertain me. My pond shall make a fitting spot for contemplation."

Adonis's lips quirked. "As you wish," he said, his voice dramatic in the way that always *hinted* at sincerity. "A princess deserves everything she wishes for, after all. The world and nothing less."

As she adjusted her skirts, Aveline sniffed. "It was your suggestion, if you recall. And perhaps not quite so much as the world."

Adonis tilted his head, looking her over with the quickest up-and-down of his eyes. Something in his gaze made Aveline shift. He looked at her like no one else did, and she knew what that meant.

"The world," he emphasised. "You deserve the world."

Aveline stared, and Adonis's lips curled more, as if he both believed his words with the entirety of his being and wished to tease her until she melted into a puddle of fabric and mist. Could both be true at once?

Aveline pushed the thought aside, and instead sent a flat look his way. "Will you lead the way to the pond?" she asked. "Or shall I?"

A guardian to lead her or a guardian to follow her?

Adonis stood, but his amusement never dimmed, his sparkle never fading. Instead, it only grew and grew and grew, like the trees of Awin: reaching for the heavens that man would never touch. Not the humans who clambered clumsily through branches and trunks, nor those who could fly like the gods themselves.

"As we both know the way," Adonis eventually said, a touch entertained, "why don't we walk side-by-side?"

Aveline's fingers twitched. "That shall suffice."

✳ ✳ ✳

The swans always danced for Aveline, as if she

were one of their own. Delicate. Beautiful. Wind-born.

But Aveline had been formed by the hands of her goddess, built in the belly of her mother, whilst her swans were little more than living statues: far closer to the clouds that carried her pond, with no sand nor mud in sight. They floated, more than swam, and had no need for food nor drink nor slumber. And yet, she adored them. And they adored her.

The pond was shielded from the rest of the kingdom by a thick ring of trees, invisible even to those in the palace. Few people knew of its presence, and Aveline did everything in her power to ensure it remained that way. Even her sister had never accompanied her, not that she had ever expressed a wish to.

It was but a short flight from Aveline's balcony, hardly enough time for even simple contemplation. The wind-drawn chariot had come to a halt upon slipping through a gap in the trees, about as far from the water's edge as the length of the pond.

Mistberries lined the branches just north of the water, their puffs of pink sugar caught between Aveline's teeth. A taste of freedom. The aroma of air-before-rain wafted through the trees, carried by mist and wind, calming the tension in her shoulders, though even they had not the ability to quash her qualms completely.

Aveline always observed the swan's dances in

such silence that their splashing of water became a song. And Adonis knew not to talk, either, though he hardly watched.

Instead, his metal gloves had been tossed across the floor of the chariot, where he sat with his legs over the edge, dangling above a cloud that would never catch one not of the Air. His mask was tied to his belt, and even his boots had been removed, like he wished not for them to be splashed by the swans that played and played.

His hands danced.

Wisps of night curled around his fingers: ink-black, but with those same speckled stars that filled his eyes and covered his skin. He stood out against the forest, as if he were but a shadow against watercolour: something that could never quite belong, yet called to her like she needed nothing more.

The swans slipped into the background of Aveline's thoughts, as if *they* were what did not belong, and she soon found herself watching her knight with equal enchantment.

His hands moved in quick, practised motions, his fingers long and nimble. He had spent his life manipulating shadows, after all, though he had grown from infancy to adulthood in Awin alone.

Uncommon. But even the kingdoms of the elements held pockets of foreign magic, dotted like ink on a painting.

In their world of Ungode, there were forty-nine magics, each in sets of seven: the Elemental, the Sinner, the Flesh, the Heart, the Force, the Mind, and the End. And every kind of magic held an island of their own, split into one-to-three kingdoms: sixty-four in total.

Ships sailed between, but not every kingdom suited every stranger.

Adonis feigned he had not noticed Aveline's stare, simply playing with his shadows like delicate clay, but those enchanting lips still quirked. Aveline found she could not look away, despite her blush, even as he finally caught her eye, nudging a squeak from her tongue.

The swirling night shot towards her, curling through the air like wind, and began to spiral around *her* fingers, too. They painted her bitten nails in sparkling shadow. Her breaths caught in her throat.

"You like my magic, swan?"

Aveline sat cross-legged on a branch that leant over her twinkling pond. She shifted, adjusting the layers of her skirt, almost dipping into that crystalline water, but just high enough to remain dry.

She cast him a flat look. "Is it not obvious, knight?"

"Humour me."

"I like all magic," she said. "Who doesn't?"

The darkness snapped back to Adonis's hands, melting into his star-speckled skin. "Humans, sometimes," he said. "And even followers despise their enemies. Fire and Ice. Dark and Light."

"Air and Storms."

"The wars are many. We hate who oppose us."

"*I* do not. What is the point?"

Adonis chuckled, his gaze drifting. He looked to the gaps of sky, barely visible between branches and leaves, and did not immediately respond. Aveline simply awaited what she knew was to come.

"You're too kind," he said, something pensive in his voice. "You don't even fear the storms?"

Her heartbeat spiked. "No."

"Huh." Adonis leant forward, head tilted back, as if wishing to catch a glimpse of something masked by the wide leaves overhead. The sun, she realised. Bright. White. The antithesis to everything he was. For a moment, he almost seemed to fear it, before his gaze returned to the shadows. "I guess I understand."

Aveline hummed, but had no answer.

None that had not already been said.

She adjusted her skirts as a swan drifted nearer. Its beak brushed the soft fabric, almost passing right through. Aveline watched with halted breath, though most of that had nothing to do with the creature.

They were surrounded by sounds, but all were soft and soothing, even with Aveline's sensitive ears. She could hardly sleep through even the lightest of storms, but her pond had never done anything but calm her. The wind alone could never set her nerves aflame, and certainly not the wind around her small, sweet-scented haven.

It never truly felt like they were alone, but it was the closest they could get under her mother's watchful eye.

The wind spiralled and hummed, more vibrant than ever, caressing her hair and brushing her cheeks, like the goddess of Air was petting the skin of her most loyal subject. Her most loyal follower in every sense of the word.

Aveline's wings twitched, faltered, and then unfurled. They stretched to their greatest length – far larger than the rest of her, as if they were the only parts of any significance – and pearl-white feathers brushed against the clouds like something physical.

Her wings folded. Her eyes slipped shut. She took a breath.

The wind laughed, tickling her tongue and tasting like sweet mistberries. Like pastries and cakes, like candied flowers and flakes of metal. Like swords and daggers and crowns and silver. Like blood and salt and hurricanes and—

Aveline's eyes shot open. She took a shuddering breath, her head snapping to look around. Frantic.

Nothing.

Nothing had changed. Everything was still.

Aveline's skin prickled. Her hair stood on end. Clouds began to gather over the pond – and not ordinary clouds, not her kin, nothing soft and white and sweet. Dark clouds, like the charcoal and stones she had seldom seen. Dark clouds like *thunder.*

Storms.

Styrme.

Aveline shot upwards, wings outstretched, and, in an instant, she was at Adonis's side. He jumped, almost tumbling into the mist below, but she caught him by the shoulder just in time. He slid backwards into safety, and the chariot trembled as he leapt to his feet.

His mask slipped from his belt. Tumbling into the abyss.

"Swan?"

Aveline tried to voice her panic – her fear she had always claimed not to have for storms, blossoming only at its mercy – but her words stuck to her throat. As her lips opened and closed, wet from the rising humidity, Adonis's look of concern mutated into a matching panic.

And then a determination. Firm.

He grabbed her arm. "Who do you need me to fight?"

She could not answer.

"Aveline. Princess. Swan! What's going on?"

Aveline raised a quivering hand and pointed up at the arrival of spiralling storm-clouds. Adonis's eyes widened. His grip tightened, before dropping entirely as he grabbed and unsheathed his sword.

A blade of shadow and a hilt of stardust.

It could never have been forged in Awin.

"What can I do?" Aveline begged.

"Flee!"

"What? Oh, I cannot possibly—"

Adonis's shoulders blocked her view of the pond. "Who is it?" he demanded, though the growing storm did not answer.

Aveline wished to grasp him by the shoulders, lift him into her arms, and fly them somewhere safe and cool and breezy – to a sanctuary, much like her pond was meant to be. But her limbs were made for laying and posing and dancing amongst swans, nothing more. She would have dropped him, and that was hardly a better fate.

She, too, would hit the ground in her efforts to rescue him.

"Adonis—"

Lightning struck the tree that leant over the pond, leaving it naught more than a charred trunk. Blackened leaves fluttered into the water, destroying the patterns made by sunbeams and swans.

The next tree was struck, cracking like a whip.

Despite the distance, shrinking with every bolt of white lightning, there was no scorching heat. Aveline felt nothing but hair on end and quivering energy, racing through her veins and making something rotten rise in her throat.

Her hand slammed over her mouth before she could curse.

Another tree was struck. Closer.

Aveline surged forward, but Adonis grabbed her by the shoulder, throwing her behind him with a strength rarely used, but clearly practised. Her back hit the chariot and she crumpled, crying out.

"Stay behind me!" was his command.

Shadows like winding vines climbed his legs. They tied him to the chariot, impossible to break, even in the midst of discord.

Aveline had no breaths in her lungs to protest with.

A woman landed on a branch halfway between the delicate chariot and the churning pond: her skin a smooth brown, her eyes a similar shade. Locks of pure white curled like bubbling waterfalls over her shoulders. A white crown was sewn into her hair with small braids.

It looked as if it had been there for a long, long time.

Aveline had seen those angular features in paintings she had thrice stumbled into, though the name slipped from her thoughts.

A princess, she knew. And a follower of the goddess of Storms.

The princess of Styrme.

Her expression was as cool, determined, as the air was quickly turning, frostbite threatening Aveline's nose and toes. Lightning crackled from the black-burnt fingers of those white-mirror gloves.

And yet, none of those sharpened features screamed cruelty. There was no malice, nor a true wish to hurt.

She was beautiful. She was furious.

She would do whatever it took.

"Give me the princess."

Adonis chuckled darkly. "Over my dead body."

The Styrmish princess did not immediately respond. Instead, she stared with a force that bore into Aveline's very soul. The moments passed like hours. An hourglass tipped. Sand refused to fall.

"I can live with that."

Her hand outstretched. Her fingers crackled with lightning.

And when everything went dark, Aveline's final thoughts were the hope she had tumbled into the shadows Adonis used to protect her.

And not the suffocating ozone stench of storm-clouds.

* * *

Aveline's eyes opened to complete and utter darkness. A darkness not of Adonis, perhaps not even of the Dark, though of that she was less certain. She knew his shadows: delicate and speckled with white. A new constellation with every dance of his fingers.

This darkness was not that.

Empty. Starless. Cold.

It took a moment – dizzying, disorienting, with acrid despair like a pebble on her tongue – before Aveline realised it was not a darkened room she had woken in, bathing her in black. It was not something her eyes would ever adjust to, but a piece of fabric wrapped around her head. A blindfold. And that only terrified her more.

Aveline was, it seemed, bound to a chair by her ankles and wrists. The ribbon- rope was thick, strong, but soft. And, though she could hardly move, she did not find herself in too dreadful a state of physical discomfort. Even the chair had been made to accommodate her wings, though she could hardly move them. The intention, she was sure.

Where was she?

Aveline could hardly think straight.

Her breaths were ragged, her lungs shredded, but, after a moment or two, she forced them to even and slow. Something bitter settled in the back of her throat: hardly fear, at that point.

The palace of home was no less of a cage.

Instead of ruminating, Aveline squeezed the arms of the chair. She must not have been there to be tortured, if the comfort of her seat was any indication. Or they would only do so if she disobeyed.

Tales of stolen royals flitted through her mind: her aunt, her grandfather, and even her eldest cousin, despite his estrangement. They never returned without scars – if not of the body, though that was typical, then of the mind. Their souls seldom remained intact.

And many more were never retrieved.

Marriage was unbreakable, and death even more so.

Aveline would not yet disobey, she decided.

Of course, she knew the fate that may still befall her. She knew what could come, what could be worse than a simple torture of whips and blades. Curses built in her throat, but she swallowed them down.

The gentle ties gave some peace.

They wished for her to be whole and unharmed; there was not a scratch on her body that she had not put there herself. They wished for their stolen princess to be *comfortable.* For now, at least.

Aveline took as even a breath as she could, and then cleared her throat. "Hello?" she called. "Your highness? Are you there?"

The quiet echoed like a discordant melody, filled only with a thunderous heartbeat and the quickened breaths of one in such tortuous peril. The wind had been cruelly snatched away.

There were no whimpers from fellow prisoners, the clanking armour of guards, nor the stench of faeces or sweat. She may not have been in a dungeon, though the air was thick and cold. Smothering.

There was nothing to suggest she was in the presence of another.

Where was she?

Aveline's lips quivered, heart trembling as if pierced on a stake. Her nails dug into the chair's wooden arms; splinters dug into the flesh of her fingers. Tears welled in her eyes like bubbles of mist.

And the blindfold was snatched away. Aveline's

tears were burned from their ducts. She met the gaze of her captor.

Jagged lightning scars burst from those dark eyes, like her irises and pupils were the bulbous bodies of white-legged spiders. And Aveline, with hurried breaths and a racing heart, could not pull her gaze away.

Those irises were almost more of prison than the chair.

The Styrmish princess leant in. Her dark fingers brushed against Aveline's cheek. The ice of her flesh broke the trance.

Aveline's heart jolted and raced with the speed of a scuttling insect, her own wings fluttering as much as they could. Desperate. She would have leant away from the touch, had she been able to.

"Are you injured?"

Aveline stared with a mouth agape and eyes as wide as could be. Her fears crashed and soared – valleys versus hills, pits versus mountains – as her blood hissed with the need to flee.

The room was deathly silent.

Her captor dropped her hand, straightening to her full height.

She was a tall, curvy woman, draped in an indigo gown, streaked with lightning and wind. A dark sky, ravaged by storm. Despite the terror it brewed, it was a dress of utmost beauty, like the clothes of a royal often were: elegant and rich. Her forearms were covered in raindrop-like loops, her ears jangling with dangling sapphires.

Her crown remained sewn to her head by the few braids in her hair, though the rest of her locks were curled and free.

There was a sword in the sheath on her belt.

"I am Princess Thalissa Gracetorn," she said, cool and serene, her voice like the music of rain. "And you have been taken to my personal tower in the grand palace of Styrme."

Aveline knew that name. How could she not?

A princess and a warrior in equal measure, of a kingdom that had not slipped from war in centuries. A follower, brewing thunder with the flick of her wrist. A woman born from lightning and storm.

Aveline took a trembling breath, and swallowed the tears that clogged her throat. She fixed her captor a firm stare. "What are you going to do to me? What have I been stolen for?"

Thalissa did not answer. Her lips pursed, pensive, as she looked over her captive like she was something to ponder.

There was no lust in her gaze, Aveline realised with relief.

But the calculation was unmatched.

Aveline's eyes darted around the room, looking not for the guards she now knew were absent – though the *why* was unknown – but some means of escape. The door was thick, pristine, and locked. But there *was* a window, casting light into the little square room.

Tall. Wide. Stained.

Glass of indigo and white. Lightning striking a spiralling tower.

Aveline wished not for that to be some kind of prophecy, but she was no fool. She knew what may come. She straightened her spine, hands squeezing the arms of the chair, and took a breath.

Would a strong kick be enough to shatter that window? She would find out as soon as she could. But that was not the only problem.

How was one who seldom left her palace supposed to find her way home across a sea that spanned miles? She had no means of navigation. She would never be able to reach Awin without the map she did not have. Where would she find search a thing?

Before Aveline's gaze could further shift, a hand grabbed her by the chin, turning her head with a force that made her gasp.

Thalissa's eyes cut into Aveline's.

"You are not to flee," she ordered. "I would catch you."

Aveline's breaths stuttered. Her eyes could not escape Thalissa's piercing pupils and irises: obsidian pearls set in dark marble. They held more secrets than even Adonis's did.

There was something almost alluring about that.

Aveline forced her eyes to close. "What do you want from me?"

"Look at me."

Teeth gritted, Aveline refused to.

The nails dug into her chin. "Look at me, Aveline."

The use of her name made Aveline jolt. Her eyes flew open, as dry as she could manage. "What do you want from me?"

Her demand trembled. A betrayal of her heart.

Thalissa watched, a peculiar expression on those sharp, beautiful features, a statue painted in only the darkest and lightest shades. She tilted her head one way, and then the other, before she whispered like the breath of a tornado. "Only what my parents wish for me."

Thalissa dropped her hand, moving backwards – footsteps like the pitter-patter of violent rain – and then spun. Her arms outstretched: a grand gesture, reaching for the sky. She looked over the bed that Aveline finally noticed, her stomach dropping.

"Only what they have always wished for, and groomed me to wish for, too," Thalissa continued, voice steady, but contemplative. "Only what has filled their every thought and every word. But a gift never given. At least not in the way I crave."

The air simmered with silence.

And Aveline realised. A fate inescapable.

She could not speak, though she wished to scream, her tongue sticking to the roof of her mouth like she had sipped too much syrup or honey. But there was nothing sickly sweet about this.

Thalissa turned back around, and Aveline caught a glimpse of blood under her captor's collar.

"They don't want it like this," Thalissa continued. "But I refuse their feeble alliances. We need not strengthen our bond with Wavun. Iycc and Ifro have not the armies we crave, not if we are to battle your ships of the sky." Her eyes glimmered with a yearning Aveline had only ever seen in her own reflection. "If I want the power I crave, I must take it."

Her hands landed on the arms of Aveline's chair, and she leant in, suddenly focused on nothing but the trembling eyes of her captive.

"I need a bride that suits *my* needs. Not what *they* want."

Aveline could hardly breathe, though that she was used to. Her chest ached as if she were dying, and she almost would have considered such a thing to be a mercy. Had her mother been right?

Had her naïve wish for freedom sent her down this path?

Aveline stared up at her captor. "You wish to bind our souls?"

"I wish to wed."

"That's the same thing, is it not?"

Thalissa raised an eyebrow.

Aveline swallowed, ignoring the bile in her throat. "Why me?"

Thalissa scoffed. "Who else? Styrme shall be mine one day." She leant in. "I want your kingdom, and you are how I am going to take it. If I win this war before it truly begins, I will have all the power I wish for. Two kingdoms to rule over. A dozen colonies in my lap. The right bride at my side. This is what I deserve, is it not?"

Aveline had nothing more to say. All that spiralled through her mind was that she *needed to escape.* For herself. For her family. For her kingdom. But how?

Thalissa watched for a moment, before pulling back. She sighed, adjusting her curls, though they and her crown were immaculate.

"There is no need to fear me, Aveline. I won't lay a finger on you, not in any sense. There is no need for it, and the consummation of marriage is nothing to force upon anybody. You will simply sit at my side for the rest of our lives, and nothing else will ever be expected of you."

Aveline's lips quivered. But she refused to weep in the presence of her captor. "Are you certain I cannot go home? You're—"

Thalissa's eyes became icy, bitter, though they did not quite reach anything cruel. Her irritation was evident, but it seemed almost... petty. It lacked a true wish to hurt. And, strangely, it lacked an understanding, too, like Aveline's fear was beginning to perplex her.

"*This* shall be your home now. And I, too, have the life of a princess, so do not expect me not to understand what I have taken you from. You are simply trading one prison for another, Aveline. How much worse is this than the alternative? A feeble marriage to a feeble ally, ending in war and a death at my hands? Is that what you crave?"

Aveline's words retreated before they could reach her lips.

"I have no one to care for," Thalissa continued. "And neither do you. I have the sisters I hardly know. I have the servants who fear me. I have the suitors my mother and father present, and I wish not to wed any of them. Have you not lived through the very same thing? Would this not be what we both need? I will rule over the kingdom of most power, and we will overtake your kingdom, which you must resent, as I do."

Aveline hardly knew the perils of war, but she knew enough to fear for her life, for her loved ones, for her people. And she knew enough to know that this needed to be stopped at all costs.

Every breeze in her veins screamed that she needed to *flee.*

Aveline had nothing to say, nothing that would not further infuriate her captor. It seemed, though, that Thalissa awaited an answer. And she was not the most patient of women.

Aveline took a slow, deep breath, though it trembled like a petal under rain. "Please... please, let me go. You can't just..."

But Thalissa could.

Her eyes hardened further, and there it was. Fury.

"Accept your fate or rot in this chair. I am unafraid of waiting, little Awinian. The weakest of us all. Do you know what my people say about yours?" She leant in, reeking of blood and old perfume. "I refuted every rumour of you, even those rooted in fact. Yet they all seem to be true."

Aveline swallowed the lump in her throat, and Thalissa's eyes only grew in their rage: as inescapable as a rumbling storm.

She turned on her heel, stomping away with the crackling of fabric and the thunder of boots against stone. She fiddled with every lock of the door, sparing a final, empty glance in Aveline's direction, before leaving and slamming it behind her.

Aveline strained to listen.

Click.

This door had an external lock, too.

Aveline had no way to flee, even if she escaped the ribbon-ropes that bound her. The window seemed the only option, and yet she doubted she held enough strength in her bones to shatter glass.

She almost swore aloud, but could not bring herself to.

Kicking as best she could, she had the chair wobbling, but it did not budge. Her wrists strained to yank themselves free, but found that to be just as much of an impossibility. And then it struck her.

If Thalissa was doing this against the wishes of her parents, without even guards to watch over her, did anyone even know Aveline was there? Thalissa did not seem the type to have trusted confidants.

Aveline's heart stuttered.

What did her parents think? What did her sister

think? What did—

Oh.

Oh, gods.

Was Adonis still alive? Would Thalissa have slaughtered him? Did his blood mingle with the ripples of her pond, forming crimson clouds and scarlet swans? Was *he* the blood on her chest?

Aveline never would have been stolen had Adonis had a choice in the matter. He would fight for her until the end.

And she would do the same, no matter the cost.

Would she ever see him again? Was there even anything left to see, anything that would not destroy her?

Aveline had hardly a hope remaining.

But she clung onto it with all that she was.

* * *

Aveline was no stranger to nightmares, haunting her without remorse, without mercy, without pause. A fresh torment whenever slumber took her into its arms and stole her away. They were as common as fallen leaves, nestled amongst death-roots and skulls.

The visions in this tower, however, had grown to an immeasurable cruelty, painting her eyelids with anguish and light.

Harsh. Sharp. Blinding.

Her pond. Empty.

Not a swan. Not a ripple. Not a sound.

Flashes of lightning. Bright. White.

Agonising.

The charred remains of the trees beyond her balcony: limbs she had once slumbered in, cradled by dreams of feathers and dawn. Destroyed.

Bodies blackened past the point of recognition.

One wore the childish skirts of her sister.

Another was sprawled across her chariot, splattered with blood as black as midnight, covering bones as white as stars, its arms outstretched and its sword ever-falling from its crumbling hand. It would never, and could never, hit the ground.

Aveline would never mistake those eyes for another: sparkling, even in death. The stars lived on without him, but they would never be the same. She watched him burn, watched him crackle and scream.

Again and again and again, until—

Her eyes shot open, wild and wide and dripping salt down swollen cheeks. Had she not been tied to the chair, she would have fallen to the floor, sprawled similarly to the corpses she would never unsee. Her back ached, but that was hardly her focus.

Was it real? Had she stumbled into a prophecy?

That was not how Aveline's magic worked.

Was *this* real? This chair and this room and this *princess*?

Aveline inhaled shakily, and then looked around with the little strength that lingered in her bones.

The bed was empty, blankets tossed aside. One of the pillows, stained with black, had been thrown from the mattress, laying halfway between Aveline and the bed. Beside the headrest, there was a small, worn table, occupied only by a single, stained mug.

Aveline drank in her surroundings as quickly as she could, having no idea how long it would take for Thalissa to reappear.

Moments, perhaps. Or even days.

She did not know which she would prefer: an eternity alone, or for her captor to return with some vicious torture, some ever-haunting monologue, those eyes that could never be escaped from.

There was a wardrobe across from the bed. Locked. There was a half-open screen, giving her a glimpse of a bowl of water and a strangely-shaped chamber pot, attached to the floor. A desk occupied half a wall, only visible when Aveline strained her neck to look over her shoulder. Books and papers were scattered across it, but none of the letters were legible, perhaps not even in the modern language of their world of Ungode. An ancient dialect, perhaps?

Aveline supposed it did not matter, especially as she caught no glimpse of any map. She would have to find one after her escape.

And then she spotted it.

A copper-red stain was splattered across one slip of paper, having fallen to the cool stone floor. It almost could have been ink, but was unmistakable, even to one unused to gore.

Aveline's breaths hitched.

She tugged at the ropes that bound her, but could not budge. Who else had Thalissa hurt? Had Aveline not been the sole captive? How many princesses had been stolen, only to be tossed aside?

Who filled Styrme's dungeons?

Aveline could gather an army the moment she returned home, guiding her knights to this prison. But she would first have to wriggle free. She would *not* be another victim. Not if she could help it.

Her struggling made no difference.

Her wings fluttered, but their movements were heavily restricted by the strange, curved back of the chair. They could only remain folded against her back, a position that had begun to ache. Her feathers itched, and though they did not quite hurt, they lingered on the borderline.

Aveline needed to fly.

She had been punished before, but never had her wings been bound for so long. Her parents had never been that cruel. They knew what it meant to worship their divine; they knew what needed to be done to stay one with their goddess. Their goddess. Their *goddess.*

The thought struck her like a blow to the head.

Aveline was not one to pray, but she was a devoted follower in her own way. She worshipped her goddess with more than blood and gold alone, though those she indulged in plenty. She used what she had been gifted, and she remained eternally grateful.

She flew – though never reaching the heavens – and she danced with the music of the wind. She even *contributed* to the wind. Her breaths could make the tiniest of tornadoes – her spiralling mist plucking leaves and rustling twigs – but that was her limit.

Flight. Exhales.

She was not the luckiest. But she was ever-grateful.

Perhaps that meant something. Perhaps her goddess paid attention.

Perhaps. Perhaps not.

There was the possibility that *Thalissa's* god would overpower Aveline's, but that was not worth pondering. It was not something a mortal would ever be able to change.

Man did not mingle with their gods.

Aveline's eyes closed, and her lips mouthed the prayers recited from infancy to adolescence. It had been three years since her eighteenth birthday – since her final, sobbing prayer – but she could not forget.

My divine.

You bless my all. My heart, my body, my soul. You carved my limbs from breeze and mist. You live amongst the heavens and know all that wander below, even those not your own.

You give me your love. You give me your flight.
You give me the winds, moulded in your image.
Bless me. Love me. Forgive me.
Bless me. Love me. Forgive me.

Bless me. Love me. Forgive me.

The final words were recited again and again and again, spilling into the icy room and filling the air with puffs of mist. Her goddess must bless her, must give her the power she needed to flee, to survive. Her goddess must love her; Aveline was carved from her feathers and bones, after all. And she must forgive her, for Aveline was, of course, impure.

All mortals were.

Aveline's mouthed words began to tremble, began to weaken, but she refused to reshape them into sobs. She prayed and she prayed until salt dripped to her lips, caught by her starved tongue. Her nose ran and her hands curled into fists, squeezing the wood of the chair with a strength that should have warped it.

What else was she to do?

She would find some way to escape.

She had to. She had to. She had to.

Aveline took a shuddering breath, and air filled her lungs, so sudden that it choked her, cutting off her tears like a knife pinning a trembling leaf. Instinctively, she exhaled, and a wind far stronger than she was capable of shot from her lips. Her chair tipped just enough to *almost* fall. It landed back on all four legs.

Aveline stared forward, open-mouthed, breaths having been stolen away. And when they did return, slow and cautious, more wind curled from her lips, cooling her throat and shaking her tongue.

Her goddess had *answered* her?

Thalissa was absent. There were no guards in the little square room, none by any of the smooth brick walls, none by this side of the door, though the other was a mystery. But that did not matter, as that was not her newfound escape route.

Aveline did not know how long she would be alone, nor how long she already had been. But that was not something to ponder.

She breathed as gently as she could, ensuring the breeze did not slip from her control. Her focus returned to the window, suddenly more a *door* than anything else. If she could break it, she could soar to safety.

Aveline was going to go home.

Aveline was going to be queen. She was going to learn every tantalising secret. She was going to set herself free.

Her stomach knotted, but her determination grew.

She closed her eyes, repeating the prayer – slipping from her tongue as if she had been made for worship and nothing more – before she reopened her eyes. She turned her head, pointing in the opposite direction to the window. Then, she parted her lips and blew. Light.

Her chair wobbled. Not enough.

She breathed softly through her nose, before opening her mouth, tongue drying in anticipation. She blew harder.

Her chair screeched across the floor, scratching the stone. It stopped halfway to the window, almost toppling. Aveline could smell the lightning and thunder and rainstorms beyond. She blew again, and the chair hit the window with a deafening crack, echoing all around and filling her skull with a pounding headache.

Aveline gritted her teeth, and turned just enough to see the window. It was not shattered, not even close. But there was a long, thin crack climbing up the middle, like lightning had burst from the earth and struck the sky instead.

Hope bubbled in her throat, mixing with nausea and fear to make a concoction she would not wish upon even her greatest enemies.

Adonis's face danced through her mind: flicking between the grin he usually wore – white-toothed and merry – and the black-bloodied face of her nightmares. The latter lingered more, especially as the moments passed. Her little sister's hesitant smile flashed alongside it.

Aveline's own face set into something cool and firm, as if she were, somehow, unafraid. She turned as much as she could, facing the window, and blew. Light. The chair slid back across the floor. She turned in the other direction, blowing harder, and the chair hit the window with another ear-splitting crack.

Again. Again. Again.

As many times as she could. As quickly as possible.

The fractured cracks spread and grew and clambered across every corner of the window, until, finally, finally, finally—

Shatter.

The glass exploded in every direction.

Aveline and her chair began to fall through the window.

The storm was deafening to an extent almost painful.

Time slowed, and the realisation that she could hardly move her wings set in, just as the arm of the chair was snatched by a dark, familiar hand. Aveline was yanked back through the window.

The goddess-enhanced wind had smeared her thoughts. Her wings had slipped from her focus, their magic relocated to her lips.

Aveline and her chair were tossed aside as one, and her head whacked against the stone floor, sending stabbing pain through her skull. She groaned, and looked up at the towering – the *furious* – Thalissa, hardly able to process that the throw had snapped most of her ropes. Both ankles were free, and one wrist.

Her wings remained trapped, but only by the angle she lay at.

Thalissa stormed over to her, snatching the front of her dress and yanking her – and the remains of the chair – upwards. Their faces were inches apart, and the scent of air-before-rain was overwhelming.

"Are you trying to kill yourself?" Thalissa

demanded. "What, in the name of the Storms, are you thinking?"

Aveline groaned, having no answer for that.

The infuriation grew. "Do you know the troubles I went through to capture you? I escaped my parent's tracking for the first time in years, knowing the punishments that would reap. They *banished* me to this disgusting part of the castle, as I knew they would."

With dazed eyes and mush for a mind, all Aveline could do was half-listen and watch. She was good at that.

"I was going to present you today," Thalissa spat. "I was going to prove that I am worthy of this kingdom, that I don't need them, that I can win this war without their guidance at all." Her lips twisted into a snarl. "I told them of a surprise, though thankfully nothing more, and you have *ruined* it. How am I to show them the precious princess I have captured, when she wishes to take her own life?"

Aveline made a soft, pained sound, and forced out the only words she could manage. "I wasn't—I wasn't trying to—to—"

Thalissa dropped her.

Pain spiked through Aveline's body as she slammed against the floor. Glass tore her dress and skin, shredding much of her remaining threads of decency. Aveline did not know which of the crunches were shards under flesh, and which were her bones.

"I know what you were trying to do. But you're too smart to think you could escape me, especially like this. Surely, some part of you knows this is all in vain?"

The words in Aveline's skull grew fuzzier. Had she hit her head too hard? It was unlikely Thalissa would provide a healer.

As if to emphasise that point, Thalissa's foot collided with Aveline's side, sending pangs of pain through every inch of flesh. Something crunched inside her, making breathing far more tortuous.

No part of Aveline was not filled with agony.

She made a desperate groan, like the whine of wounded prey. Her vision blurred, and she could hardly even see Thalissa. A distorted shadow. A blur, much like the watercolour mists of home, but far darker. Crueller. An expression utterly incomprehensible.

The details were far from Aveline's focus. She only wished for an end to the pain. How would she save herself in this state?

Thalissa crouched, grabbing the front of Aveline's dress again, pulling her up, but not quite so far. Aveline could see nothing but those harsh, desperate eyes. Dark. Streaked with vibrant lightning.

Not so unlike Adonis's stars. But a cruel mockery.

Aveline's heart ached more than the rest of her.

Thalissa did not speak for another full minute, and Aveline's daze made it last hours. Thalissa dropped her.

"I shall return with a potion of healing. And you would do good not to try and escape again, or I shall pluck you like a quail." Thalissa paused, and, for a moment, her blurred form returned to something almost clear – haloed by the glow of lightning striking earth, just beyond the window – though the rest of Aveline's vision remained fuzzy. "Don't think I haven't taken precautions. The storms beyond my window will rip you to pieces. And I know *exactly* how to track you."

With that, Thalissa turned on her heel. She marched to the open door, slamming it shut behind her, and locked it with a click that made Aveline's ears ring.

For a while, there was nothing to do but wallow and groan, until her mind focused enough to fix on the window. A dark, open mouth with jagged teeth of white and blue. She could fit through it again, and her wings were finally free. She could *fly*.

Aveline tried desperately to clamber to her feet, tried desperately to flap her wings, but the moment her body lifted from the floor, she collapsed into a puddle once more.

And darkness overtook her again.

* * *

It took two days for Thalissa to return.

Two days of agony.

The pain faded into a steady ache: manageable,

perhaps, in better circumstances, but Aveline had never before been in such peril. And, it seemed, this kingdom was doing everything in its power to torment her.

The lack of window had attracted only the worst of storms.

Rain sprayed across everything, no matter the proximity to that side of the room, making the scattered shards sparkle. Thunder rumbled and snarled like a beast, almost impossible to sleep through. Lightning threatened to destroy her as it crackled and screamed. Far too close.

Was every day in Styrme so tortuous, and Aveline had simply been protected by the window she never should have destroyed? Or did this all come from Thalissa's hands?

Aveline could not leapt through that jagged mouth, as she would fall right into the belly of that thunder-formed beast. Impossible to see through, impossible to break through, even if she aimed to soar to the safety above the clouds.

She would never survive, especially as her body was riddled with bruises and cuts. Her fingers trembled, her feet speckled with crimson, and her head pounded like that was where her heart now resided.

And she was incurably lonely.

Aveline eagerly awaited the return of her enemy, though she bitterly despised every ounce of it. She watched the door like a sharp-eyed hawk, hardly breathing, as if noise would frighten her captor away.

And when Thalissa *did* return, Aveline fell to her knees at her feet – head spinning, thoughts far from coherent – to the shock of one who may never have seen such desperation in her path.

Aveline despised it. But that was all she was anymore. Desperate.

Thalissa stared, and then sighed.

She closed and locked the door behind her, and dropped a tray onto the floor. It held a small, corked bottle – filled with something viscous and white – and the remains of a marvellous feast. A misshapen chunk of cheese, hastily separated from something far bigger, its blueish veins like jagged lightning. A slice of thick, rich bread, a bite taken from one corner. A bird bone half-gnawed, but with just enough scraps of meat to make it more than simple food for pests.

Aveline had never before wished to devour something so greedily, but as she reached to grab the meat, a boot landed on her hand, pinning it to the floor and pulling a whine from her lips. She looked up at Thalissa with widened eyes, and Thalissa glared like Aveline's every move infuriated her.

"The potion first," she snapped. "It took me too long to find, so you're not wasting it."

Aveline stared, before she came to her senses and snatched the bottle from the tray. It was cool, damp, like fresh mist, and Aveline did not hesitate. She uncorked it with her teeth, spat the cork aside, and guzzled the potion in one go.

Thick. Sickly. Cold.

Familiar.

Aveline gagged, but managed to keep it down as she scrubbed at her mouth with her sleeve. Then, she looked back up at Thalissa. Her silence begged for permission to eat.

Thalissa watched for a few careful moments.

The potion began to set in, Aveline's mind clearing and her aches dissolving into fog. She could feel the torn flesh of her feet healing, though the stains of blood remained. It did not quite cure all, her anguish lingering, but Aveline was grateful.

Was her captor really so cruel, if she cured the one she had hurt?

Aveline almost slapped herself across the face.

She was no freer than before.

Thalissa finally nodded. She removed her boot from Aveline's hand, and crossed the room with quick strides. She sat on the bed, neatening the blankets Aveline had formed into a nest. It seemed she no longer cared for the actions of her prisoner, and Aveline began to eat.

She gobbled with the ferocity of a wild beast, getting grease in the hair that had long-since fallen from its braid. And, when she was done, she lapped up the juices and crumbs with her tongue.

Then, she sat back on her heels and turned to Thalissa, who was, finally, looking at her again.

A dark shiver danced up and down Aveline's

spine. She could not move an inch, as if she were a flower rooted to a branch: strong enough to resist being plucked by the breeze, but any hand would have been able to snatch her with ease.

She swallowed, thick, and folded one hand over the other in her lap.

She did not speak. Thalissa did not, either.

Instead, she slipped from the bed, marched to the window, and turned over her closed hand. As she unfurled her fingers, she revealed a tiny shard of glass, nestled in her palm.

Aveline watched, enraptured, as Thalissa tossed it into the air, before catching it between two fingers, unafraid of the potential slicing of flesh. She held it up to where the window had been.

Lightning shot from it, stretching to the jagged remains of the glass, like cracks through the darkening sky. It made no sound, but Aveline's skin prickled. Then, what had once been a window shimmered.

Sunlight on a crystal pond.

A stone settled in Aveline's gut, and the food she had devoured threatened to rise and spill back through her lips. She forced it down.

Aveline almost did not notice when Thalissa released the shard, even as it remained in place. But what she *certainly* noticed was the silence that smothered everything. It was like the storm had been vanquished, though it had not. It raged as if battling the sky, rain splattering through where the window should have been, but it was silent.

Magic of Silence, Aveline supposed.

It was far from peaceful, far from still. Thunder shook the tower like it had been grasped by the hand of a giant, flashes of lightning turning half the room white. But it was silent.

Thalissa turned back to Aveline, and the prisoner tensed, ready to sink her teeth into her captor's flesh. But she restrained herself, even as Thalissa marched over to her, crouched, and caught her by the wrist, dragging her to her feet.

"You are not to speak," she ordered. "I am going to sleep, and you would be wise to do so, too. We have matters to discuss at sunrise."

Thalissa released her, and Aveline barely managed to remain standing. She wobbled from lingering hunger, but her outstretched arms maintained her balance. The determination she was regaining kept her from crumbling into dust.

As if Aveline had returned to a state of irrelevance, Thalissa walked past her, stopping at the foot of the wardrobe. She pressed her palm to the padlock, and the door swung open as if delighted to obey.

The clothes inside were dark and beautiful, as if plucked from storm-speckled nights. Indigo and navy, with spots and slashes of coin and snow. When Thalissa began to change – on her own, to Aveline's bewilderment – Aveline realised she should look away.

She turned, and began to fiddle with her fingers. Her next steps… what would they be?

The window was her only method of escape. That was irrefutable.

But how was she to calm the storms? And how would she do so before she was taken from this tower and wed? Thalissa was no fool. She would not be so easy to trick.

Aveline bit her tongue, the copper taste almost grounding.

As she listened to the rustling fabric of her captor undressing, her mind raced like a pegasus, finally clearer than the two days prior. Her thoughts were cacophonous but she sailed like a swan in a tsunami.

Should she battle her captor? Should she threaten the woman into letting her go? How was she to cross the sea?

Would passage on a ship be worthwhile to consider? She had no blessed coins, not on her person, only jewellery now scattered across a glass-speckled floor, dotted with rainwater and mist. Would a promise of blessed coins on arrival be enough? That, or pirates who traded with people and gold would find her instead, and drag her to a fate no better than what Thalissa had promised.

Should she pray to her goddess once more? It had not worked since her near-escape, though she had begged and begged and begged, screaming until her throat was on fire.

The thought of awaiting rescue remained the most bitter.

Aveline tried not to think about the only one who knew who had taken her, the only one with any hope of guiding soldiers in a mission of rescue. What had happened to him?

Taking a slow breath, Aveline turned. She lay eyes on Thalissa halfway out of her dress, her undergarments a thick, stark white, made of cloth and strange bones.

"What did you do to Adonis?"

Thalissa cast a look back over her shoulder, speckled with jagged white scars, unperturbed by the witness of her state of undress. "Who?"

For a moment, the words stuck in Aveline's throat.

Thalissa raised an eyebrow.

Aveline's nails dug into the flesh of her palms, as sharp as splintered glass. "My knight," she said. "What did you do with my knight?"

Thalissa pursed her lips. She turned away once more, wriggling out of the bones that squeezed her. "You cannot care about someone not of our status. You are to be my wife, Aveline. You should have no concern for an unimportant."

"He *isn't* unimportant!"

A glare was cast over Thalissa's shoulder, filled with a ferocity that had Aveline's heart jumping. No words left those dark-painted lips, and Aveline's own thoughts retreated, slipping back down her throat.

If she had not been such a coward, perhaps...

Aveline turned away, and allowed Thalissa to

continue dressing in peace. The peace that Aveline had not been granted.

Her hands curled into fists, though fighting Thalissa was the very last thought to come to mind – for now, at least. Aveline knew her own strength, and Thalissa had fought her so easily before.

If an attempt to battle would have brought Adonis back, she would have pounced in a heartbeat. But that was not the case.

She would have to find some other escape.

The only thing that brought comfort – a small, curling comfort, like a seed nestled in a heart that pumped fear and pain like blood – was the dawning realisation that if Thalissa did not consider Adonis important, perhaps that meant he was not important enough to be killed. Perhaps it meant she had slaughtered him without remorse, but Aveline had to protect that new hope with everything she was.

Hope was the only way she would survive.

Aveline took a breath, unfurled her fists, and then sat on the floor, right beside the tray of food that had not been enough. She crossed her legs underneath her, folded her hands in her lap, and waited.

Thalissa said nothing else.

She finished dressing, closing her wardrobe with a slam, and Aveline finally looked to her again, watching as she crossed the room, blowing out every candle on the desk but one: each that glowed far brighter and longer than any ordinary candle would have. The kingdom of Lignet – worshippers of Light – sold their blessed candles and lanterns like they were as common as leaves in a kingdom of forests.

It was a small comfort that Aveline would not be bathed in darkness.

That would have pained her beyond belief.

Aveline watched, silent, as Thalissa stepped over to her bed, climbed inside, and covered herself with the thick blankets necessary to slumber in a kingdom of chill. Aveline's skin prickled.

But Thalissa did not yet close her eyes, and instead locked gazes with her. "You are not to attack me," she whispered. "If you do, you shall never escape. The storms around my tower will live on without me. You will die if you flee through the window."

"Understood."

"If you are not hunted by my guards and slaughtered at my people's feet, you will remain forever trapped. I charmed the locks with blood."

Aveline's gaze flicked to the door, and there it was. Invisible to one not looking just right. A smooth, small fingerprint: a red so black it bordered on blue, like ink had replaced Thalissa's blood.

Aveline's eyes darted back to her captor, who watched with the stillness of one carved from obsidian.

"Sleep," Thalissa ordered. "I have preparations to

make tomorrow."

"What preparations?"

Thalissa shot her a glare, refusing to utter another word, though Aveline's mind screamed to know more of her fate. Her nails left indents in her palms, but instead of inciting battle, or even simply scowling, Aveline took a deep breath, and nodded.

A moment passed. Two. Three.

Thalissa's eyes slipped shut – her white eyelashes shimmering in the candlelight – and she seemed to drift into slumber in an instant.

Aveline could not trust this.

She stared – breaths held, limbs tense – awaiting an attack she was not so sure would come. Should she attack first? Thalissa was *defenceless*, at least until she woke.

Aveline eyed the shards of glass, and even the cracked remains of her jewelled pins, each glimmering in the amber light. They were wet from rain, likely slippery, but if Aveline was careful, she could find a piece of suitable shape and size, dry them on her dress, before pouncing.

She could slit the throat of a slumbering enemy. Anyone could.

A terrible thought. A tantalising thought.

Or perhaps, at least, she could *threaten* Thalissa.

Aveline tried to stand, but her limbs failed her, wobbling until she fell into a puddle. A quiet curse slipped from her tongue, but she had always known her own strength. Why was she surprised?

Thalissa would disarm her in a moment.

And, even if Aveline *did* kill her, there was no way of escaping, not through the storms, nor from the guards who would tear her to shreds.

She had to. But how?

"Fuck," Aveline muttered.

She swallowed, thick and pained, dislodging the tears that clogged her throat. She then pushed her agonies aside. And, slowly, keeping her eyes on Thalissa – dimly lit, but haloed by amber – she slid backwards until she hit a wall: as far from her foe as she could reach.

How long would it take her people to realise she was in Styrme?

They must suspect their most violent enemies of being the culprits. But if nobody but Thalissa knew she was there, would a war with those *actually* in power even lead to the reveal of Aveline's taking?

Would Awin and Styrme destroy one another? Would a war flourish and shrivel before Aveline could be found? Would she rot here?

No. No, she would not.

Aveline was going to escape this tower, no matter what it took. She would return to Elodie and Adonis. She would return home as a hero to her people, as one who had survived the brutality of the enemy. Her mother would finally trust her. Her people would finally know her.

Though her gut trembled with butterflies and nausea, Aveline kept a tight grip on the hope in her heart. She squeezed her hands into fists as if that was what held it in place.

Then, she closed her eyes, wings curling around her body, though they itched and twitched and begged to be unfurled.

"I can do this," she mumbled. "I'm going to… I'm going to be okay."

Aveline pressed the heels of her palms into her eyes, blocking out the remaining streaks of candlelight. Black mist filled her gaze.

"I can do this. I'm going to survive."

She swallowed her nausea.

"I'm going to see them again. And I'm going to be free."

Crack.

Aveline cried out, wings unfurling just in time for her to see the second bolt of lightning strike the floor in front of her. She jolted, looking to the bed, and found Thalissa staring intensely.

Her hand was outstretched – the only part of her, besides her face, that was not smothered by a blanket – and Aveline could see the lingering light as it faded.

For a moment, there was nothing.

And then Thalissa rolled over, leaving Aveline to pray to herself and her goddess, just, this time, in silence.

❖ ❖ ❖

The silencing shard, cast the night prior, had

faded and fallen. The whistles of wind and the pounding of rain and the grumbles of starved thunder filled the room. Perhaps the first would have brought comfort, filling Aveline's mind with the peace that wind often brought, but nothing could calm her: not her blood, not her magic, not her goddess.

Instead, Aveline found herself shivering in a dress too thin, unable to focus on anything but the storm's eternal torment. It echoed through her skull like a vicious headache.

Would she ever grow accustomed to it?

She hoped she would not have to.

"If you're not going to eat that, I shall take it back."

Thalissa's snap dragged Aveline from her hope-starved mind.

Her eyes focused on the plate of food in front of her, where she sat, on the floor, cross-legged and trying not to puke. It was not the meal itself that made her wish to vomit, though it was hardly appealing, cold and composed entirely of scraps. Instead, what *did* make her queasy was the realisation that Thalissa could have done *anything* with it.

Potions were attainable in this kingdom, though rare. And there *were* magics of Love, Lust, and Desire.

Would it not be easier to remould Aveline's mind than convince her with words alone? Thalissa certainly seemed the type to consider it. And she had not been there when Aveline had woken, had not come to collect her captive for whatever preparations she had sworn to enact.

Where had she gone?

Aveline took a slow, careful breath, and shook her head, her loose, half-wet hair hanging in strings like blanched worms. She shifted backwards, brushing glass aside, and smothered the hunger that lingered in her grumbling stomach.

She would not become a mindless pet.

Thalissa scowled, dropping her own plate across from Aveline's, and then slid along the floor so she was closer to her captive. Though Aveline was as tense as a string pulled taut, she did not further flee.

Thalissa snatched her fork from the floor, pointing it as if she wished to impale her, before she flipped it, and instead pointed at Aveline with the handle. Filled with caution, Aveline simply stared.

"Take it."

Aveline did so. And did nothing else.

Thalissa rolled her eyes, leaning in. She prodded the arm that held the fork, and Aveline inhaled through her teeth, almost dropping it.

"Take any piece of food from your plate and give it to me."

"Excuse me?"

"I'll eat it, and you'll know I haven't tried to poison or enchant you."

Aveline stared, wide-eyed and empty-throated. Thalissa stared back. Neither moved, not an inch, not until Thalissa's expression twisted into one of greater infuriation.

"Do it," she snapped. "I will not allow my bride to starve."

"You cannot blame me for my assumptions."

"Can I not?"

The snap silenced Aveline's tongue. After a moment, she inhaled, exhaled – testing for the presence of a blessing, though nothing came of it – and then obeyed. She stabbed a lump of potato with her fork, and handed Thalissa the utensil.

Their fingers brushed. Aveline shivered.

Thalissa did not react, except to place the potato on her tongue, chewing it carefully, before handing the fork back to Aveline. Thalissa gave her a pointed look, and swallowed.

"There," she said. "Eat."

Aveline looked between Thalissa, the fork, and her plate.

Could she trust this? Who would, in her shoes?

Her stomach grumbled and her jaw twinged. Aveline would not escape with no strength in her bones. She needed *something*, or she might as well accept death as her only fate.

She gave in.

The food may have tasted rich, delicious, like the feasts she had grown so accustomed to – though saltier, with more plants of the earth and chewier meat – had it not been cold and clearly what no one else would touch. But Aveline's belly ached, and she supposed she had to take what she could get. She would not escape in such a state.

Thalissa watched through it all. She said nothing, not yet, not until Aveline was on the verge of licking her plate clean.

"What are your thoughts on my kingdom?"

Aveline blinked, startled.

But Thalissa, it seemed, had decided to be patient. Even as Aveline had nothing yet to say, Thalissa waited with nothing more than a look of simple expectation: one eyebrow raised, one palm on the floor.

Aveline swallowed.

What could she say? She knew little of Styrme's internal affairs, little she had not thought to be rumours. They were cruel and subtle, sneaking into their colonies and infecting them from the inside out.

Styrme was said to have sicknesses that could turn one into thunder and smoke. Slow. Agonising. Inevitable.

Aveline knew of the mountains and the valleys, had seen paintings of them all, but that was not what Thalissa was asking for. And though Aveline was well-accustomed to deception, she was tired.

"I... don't know much about your culture, I'm afraid."

Thalissa frowned. A curious disapproval. "Our kingdoms are on the brink of war, and you, heir to the throne, have nothing more to say?"

"I'm not told very much."

Thalissa did not answer.

Aveline was almost ready to spit in her face. "If I had more to tell you, I would. But I do not, I'm afraid. Find your insight elsewhere."

Her gaze fixed onto the floor, dotted with puddles and frost.

Silence.

Aveline's eyes darted back to Thalissa, finding her gaze on the storms beyond the window. Lightning reflected in Thalissa's dark eyes: as enrapturing and inescapable as this and any other tower.

"My parents tell me what they deem necessary," Thalissa finally said: cool and serene. "The culture of the enemies. The histories of our great kingdom. The actions of rulers present and past. But they do not allow me any choice. I cannot pick my path." Her words were bitter, and she finally looked to Aveline with an expression not of malice, but something far stranger. "I suspect your parents are much the same."

Aveline took a slow, careful breath.

How did one balance honesty with fear?

"Yes," she whispered. "They are."

The pair slipped into silence once again.

Aveline inhaled as quietly as she could: a leaf caught between a finger and a thumb, given just enough freedom to tremble in the wind, but never to escape. She exhaled. "Why don't you leave?"

Thalissa caught her gaze. "Why didn't you?"

"I don't want to." Aveline fiddled with her hands. "I may crave a little freedom, but I must give my kingdom the queen it deserves, no matter what I must sacrifice to do so."

Thalissa huffed, but it bordered on bitter merriment. "It appears we understand each other more than we thought. I *will* give my kingdom the queen it deserves, no matter who I must sacrifice to do so."

Aveline flinched.

Thalissa lifted the cup beside her plate, taking a sip. When she lowered it, her dark lips were stained with red. Aveline shuddered as if Thalissa really had been guzzling blood, though she now suspected that not to be one of her captor's favoured pastimes.

"You and I have much in common," Aveline muttered, hardly louder than the wind. "We are both far too loyal."

Thalissa's expression twitched. She placed her cup beside her, and, without warning, shifted so she was on her knees. She reached out, taking one of Aveline's hands into her own. Though Aveline's heart jumped and breaths hitched, she made no move to pull away.

Thalissa lifted the hand to her lips and kissed it.

Crack.

The lightning was comparable to an ember. It set her skin aflame, leaving a charred mark behind, but it did not hurt. It, instead, made Aveline's heart ache with bitter memory.

And churn with a silent hatred as well.

"We shall make a fitting queen and consort," Thalissa said. "And I swear I shall hide nothing from you. The kingdom of Styrme will prosper, and we will win this war."

Aveline's breaths stuttered.

She knew what winning this war would mean for those of Awin: for her mother, her father, her sister. Adonis. She knew what sat on the horizon, like a bone-crunching bird, soaring to catch a fallen corpse.

Aveline swallowed the tears that clogged her throat.

Would they make a fitting queen and consort?

"Yes," she said. "I suspect we will."

Aveline would have to escape quickly, lest that become the case.

❊ ❊ ❊

The night came quickly, unlike every night prior, where Aveline had wasted away the hours of daylight praying to her goddess, watching the window, and preening her feathers as best she could. She had cycled between each, repetitive and slow, until the day had slipped into darkness, plagued with nightmares and plight.

This time, however, Thalissa remained at her side.

She gave no sympathy. Her words were never gentle nor kind – as cool as a snowstorm, as wind in the dead of night – but they lacked a heart-born cruelty. Her every sentence swung between wistful and sincere, and ignorant and unashamed.

Thalissa had a lot to say, especially to someone who could do nothing but listen and placate her.

Aveline almost had not noticed when midnight had fallen, not until it finally hit her that the room had faded into candlelit black. Though the storms raged on, the sky was a wall of obsidian and ink, often slashed by streaks of white lightning.

The storm-clouds smothered the night's usual lights.

Aveline swallowed the lump in her throat, and looked from the window to Thalissa, who had spent the last minute or so in contemplative silence. Thalissa met her gaze, flicked to look at the empty night, before she turned to Aveline once more.

In the amber candlelight, her white curls shimmered like a cloud set aflame. A glimpse of home, almost.

Aveline's shoulders tensed. How long would it be until she returned?

She craved metal hands and sweet mistberries more than anything.

Thalissa stood, stretched like her limbs ached, and then looked to the bed. "If I want to awaken early enough to present you to my parents, I should slumber now," she said, empty of anything indicative of her innermost thoughts. "They rise with the sun, and expect me to follow suit. And

I have made certain… arrangements. Tomorrow, my plans shall be enacted. Finally."

Aveline's stomach dropped. "Tomorrow?"

Thalissa quirked a brow as if lingering between derision and bemusement. "Yes," she said. "Tomorrow."

As if Thalissa had struck her again, every breath slipped from Aveline's lungs, akin to being viciously squeezed. Was she to drown, though amongst only air? The home of her soul, the blood of her goddess. Her heart ached like it, too, was being mangled by her foe.

Tomorrow. Tomorrow. *Tomorrow.*

Aveline would never get a moment alone. Aveline would never get a moment to escape. Aveline would never…

Her lower lip trembled.

She bit down on her tongue, painting copper across the inside of her cheeks. Then, she forced her shoulders to relax. As Thalissa turned back and met her gaze, Aveline straightened. "Of course. Sleep well."

Thalissa watched, something unreadable crossing her face.

Her dark eyes darted to her bed, lingering, before returning to Aveline. She smoothed her hands over her skirt. "Only peasants and prisoners slumber on floorboards. Join me. Nothing will happen, of course, but as my fiancée, you shall have to adjust to my presence."

"Am I… not a prisoner?"

"You are to be my bride. This is now *your* home, too. Whilst you must remain at my side, you are no prisoner."

Aveline bit her tongue, suppressing the retort that she most certainly *was* a prisoner. She was not permitted to leave, to contact her most beloved, to even know of his fate. She was to be some precious object. A trinket. And she would be tracked if she, somehow, fled.

A gilded cage was almost worse.

A gilded cage was all she had ever known.

How different was this? She had spent hours pondering it, but never quite so deeply. If Aveline was to remain, all she would have done was flit from one tower to another. An old cage to one polished anew.

It was already almost *better* than the suitors she had been made to consider. They expected far more of her, the parts of her body she wished not to share with any keeper. Her lips, her breasts, the valley between her thighs. And she would have been just as unable to flee.

Aveline's wings twitched, but she ignored their silent demands.

The only significant difference was that a spouse of the Air would likely permit her guard to remain at her side. They would have no reason to cast him away, let alone…

A shiver scraped her spine. But instead of quivering, she remained firm. "Of course."

Thalissa nodded. Satisfied.

Those eyes like rich, liquid bronze bore into a grey like soft, precious clouds. Treasures seldom seen in the other's kingdom. They remained locked for a few moments, and Aveline's heart raced faster.

Thalissa stepped back. "I will find you suitable clothes once we wake. Would you like similar shades? A gown of cream and pink, and white jewellery? We cannot quite recreate the misty effect, but that's a minor detail. And everything shall be made to accommodate your wings." At Aveline's nod, she seemed satisfied. "You shall wear the symbols of our kingdom, too. And I shall find you a ring."

A shackle was a far more apt term.

Aveline's eyes prickled, but, while Thalissa's gaze shifted, she raised her fists and scrubbed away the stinging salt. She was not to cry in the presence of her enemy. That was a weakness ungranted.

She took a breath. "Of course."

"We'll wed soon," Thalissa continued. "Once we are wives, your fate can be revealed to your parents, sister, and subjects, giving them ample time to weep over your absence before we attack. How long are periods of mourning in your kingdom?"

Aveline clenched her jaw almost hard enough to shatter bone. The glass shards grew more and more appealing. She stood. "It depends on the circumstances, I suppose. I'm not dead, so..."

"Understood." Thalissa waved her hand

dismissively. "I shall spare you the details of our weapons, armies, ships. Those are secrets I shall not grant you. But we *shall* be triumphant. Awin and its colonies will be under our control, and Arelc and Alyro will be next."

Secrets. Secrets. *Secrets.*

"What is with that look on your face?"

Aveline swallowed. She clasped her hands behind her back to keeping her fingers from morphing into claws. "It is nothing, Thalissa."

"You are not to lie to me."

Aveline scoffed. Her eyes fixed to the floor, her toe tracing shapes in the puddle beside her. "I am to lie to everyone, Thalissa. That is all I am, as that is all I am given." Her bitter heart was undisguised.

The whistling wind grew in tempo. Its violence had Aveline's hair whipping like weapons and hitting her neck.

Both her breaths and Thalissa's were smothered.

Aveline bit down on her tongue, before raising her head once again.

Thalissa stared down at her, silent and still. The seconds passed like hours, stretching into infinity. And then Thalissa turned away. "If Styrme is put in an unfavourable position of surrender – though this shall never come to pass – your people shall be unable to hurt me, lest they destroy your heart in the process."

Marriage was a bond never broken.

That was what the gods had decreed.

Aveline took another breath, before she nodded.

As Thalissa turned away, she grabbed the sides of her dress, balling her hands into fists of fabric, and *squeezed*, as if that would do anything to assist her wailing heart. Her legs stung with new scratches, though in the back of her mind she wished only to worsen them.

Thalissa looked to her again. Aveline's hands fell back to her sides.

Without another word, Thalissa marched over to her wardrobe, throwing it open, and began to undress.

Aveline turned away, though she supposed it was pointless, as Thalissa cared not for whether she was ignored or observed. Still, she waited for Thalissa to close the wardrobe before she took a peek, finding her dressed in shades of midnight and cobalt: a simple nightgown that trailed along the floor. Her crown remained braided in her hair, and Aveline's gaze fixed onto it.

Did she always wear that?

Aveline had yet to see her without it, so she supposed that must have been the case. That pristine crown and those tight white curls were perfect and pure, no matter the moment. She must have had several servants who fixed it whenever it went askew.

Thalissa gave her an odd look. "What is it?"

Aveline jolted, face burning. She scrambled to find something to say, but her mind emptied of everything but the truth. "Why do you always wear your crown?"

Though there was no way she could have seen it at that angle, Thalissa's eyes flicked upwards. She shrugged. "My parents forbade its removal. It's a spell, anyway, with origins I am unaware of, though I suspect it comes from Custrose or Colesse with their magic of Costume. It is a weight I have grown used to." Thalissa paused. "And you shall have to, as well, I assume. They'll likely enforce it."

Aveline's eyes widened, hands flying to touch her tangled locks. The pins had long since scattered and shattered, indistinguishable from the glass across the floor. Her hair was greasy, filthy, and wet.

"All right," she said, nauseous. "I can manage that."

She had to escape first.

Thalissa gave a short nod of approval, and then turned back to the bed, striding over to it. "Come," she ordered. "Now is the time for slumber. May you extinguish every candle but one?"

Aveline nodded, scrambling to do so – every lung-born breeze against flame sending thoughts of escape throughout her – before all that remained was the one at the end of the desk. A short, round candle: black, with spots of white embedded in the wax.

Aveline's heart stuttered, her face crumpling, before she forced herself to focus on the cool, wet stone beneath her feet. She smoothed over her features, banishing her despair. Then, she turned, looking to Thalissa, who had already descended into the bed's thick blankets.

The thought of joining her made thunder brew in Aveline's belly.

The thought of slitting her throat did the very same.

She believed Thalissa's claims of nothing terrible awaiting her, though the rips in Aveline's clothes left her far more exposed than she had ever wished to be. But Thalissa had already proven that she was unafraid of violence, whether warranted or not.

Gods. What was Aveline to do?

Swallowing her dread, Aveline tiptoed over to the bed, dodging the stained, sparkling shards across the floor. It would have been impossible to spot them, had they not reflected every flash of lightning like the tiniest of mirrors.

An underfoot crunch would be all it took to slice her flesh into ribbons. But a careful hand could pluck a shard from the floor and use it to cut something else.

The throat or the belly or the wrists of her captor. The throat or the belly or the wrists of herself. An escape.

But she could not betray Adonis in this way.

A strange thought struck her, sliding to the forefront as if slick with blood and rain. If Adonis lived, perhaps she could convince her bride to fetch her knight, to allow him to follow her into this new life, despite the war. He was not of Air, after all. He was not Thalissa's natural foe.

Aveline revoked the idea, refusing to test it on her tongue.

She would not do that to Adonis. That was not even to be considered, simply another yearning she could never act upon. She would not take his freedom. He needed that more than anything.

But she *could* ensure his safety, if that remained an option.

A strange relief overwhelmed her.

Did she... actually have power over this? Could she save the ones she cared for most, simply by sacrificing her freedom?

Aveline had never had any freedom in the first place.

In the morning, she would make that request, she decided. She would behave: be the obedient princess everyone expected her to be. The obedient bride. A beauty to bask in the gazes of others, but never to speak unless those in power deemed it a necessity.

She would behave. She would ensure certain people would be exempt from the violence of war. Adonis. Elodie.

Aveline would never be able to carve such a fate for her parents, but she would rescue those she could. And she would, in some way, win.

Aveline climbed into bed beside Thalissa, and found the other woman had shifted to the very edge of her side, leaving Aveline with more than enough room, even with the wings that sprouted from her back. Still, Aveline ensured *she* was also at the very edge of her own side, leaving the tips of her feathers to touch the floor behind her.

They did not speak, but remained so close that, even with the storm battling itself, sending water across the sparkling floor, their breaths overcame it all. Thalissa's were heavy and harsh, and if Aveline strained to listen – her own breaths smothered by her hand – she could hear the crackle of lightning in the back of Thalissa's throat. She could almost taste that sizzling heat, though Thalissa's every other organ and limb radiated a permeating chill.

Staying as silent as she could, Aveline listened to Thalissa's breaths deepen and slow. They lost their harsh, deliberate tinge.

She was asleep.

Aveline managed to relax, just a little, and burrowed further under the blankets: far more preferable than the ice of the window, shattered by her own idiocy. Her eyes screwed tightly shut, and pictures painted themselves across her fluttering eyelids.

A hand, speckled with stars, reaching out and taking her own into its palm. A smile with teeth that sparkled.

Over his dead body.

His last response echoed in her ears. As midnight crept closer, anything but silent and still, that was all that filled her mind. Despair. She could think of nothing else. She could think of no one else.

Aveline bit down on the flesh of her palm.

She refused to banish her hope.

Adonis may live. She knew that.

Aveline's eyes remained closed as she forced herself to relax, forced herself to focus on one thing and one thing only. The wind.

Amongst the rumbling thunder and the rain against rooftops and the crackle of lightning, there remained the sweet singing of the wind. A serenade handcrafted by her most beloved goddess.

Even in Styrme, her Air-divine remained. She sang a mournful tune, like she missed the princess snatched from her grasp. Though there were no words, Aveline found herself almost *understanding* that strange, discordant melody.

A warning. A regret. A wish.

A lack of power born from too much.

Aveline could not discern anything more, nor did she understand why her goddess refused to help. But, she supposed, this was all she really needed. All she needed was the *presence* of her goddess, making her wings twitch and heart flutter. It brought a strange peace to Aveline's wretched mind. She took a slow, mournful breath.

"I will protect you, Elodie," she whispered. "I will protect you, Adonis, if you truly remain. And, my goddess, I beg of you. Save my kingdom, if your heart desires it."

Aveline listened to the wind and the wind alone, and her mind began to drift, began to dissolve into something fuzzy. Her tears slowed, her breaths calmed, and sleep slipped over her, accompanied not only by the storm, but by the movements of the blanket beside her.

❉ ❉ ❉

She floated.

She drifted amongst clouds, above her pond, amidst her trees.

Weightless. Empty. Peaceful.

A feather. A breeze.

A dove. A swan.

A pawn and a princess and a prisoner.

Dreaming. Dreaming. Dreaming—

Aveline was torn from her mind by a pair of hands – fingers long, thin, and as sharp as pointed blades – grasping her by the shoulders and shaking her violently. She, of course, woke screaming, but a hand slammed over her mouth, silencing her in an instant.

It took a little longer for her eyes to clear, especially in the dim, foggy light, but soon her vision was filled with a dark face, jagged lightning pulsing from black-lined eyelids.

Thalissa.

That should not have quashed Aveline's fears, but it did.

It was only Thalissa.

Aveline looked to her captor with widened eyes. She raised a quivering hand, and carefully pushed

Thalissa's off her face, taking harsh, irregular breaths. "What are y—"

Thalissa hushed her through clenched teeth.

Aveline's frustration sparked. She sat up, fists furling and wings twitching. "Thalissa, what in the heavens are you doing?"

In lieu of giving an answer, Thalissa cast a glance back over her armour-clad shoulder at the door that did not budge, firmly bolted and locked and stained with dark scarlet.

Then, she looked to Aveline once more. "You need to leave."

Leave. Leave. *Leave.*

Aveline had seldom heard those words before.

They struck her to her core, far more violent and nauseating than any punch could have been. She stared. "Leave—leave where?" Aveline's heart sank into her stomach. "Are you... sending me to some dungeon?"

How was she to make the deals she craved if she was banished to a dungeon? If she was demoted to a pure prisoner, not simply a bride-to-be, would she have the power to protect Elodie and Adonis?

Aveline could not breathe.

Thalissa shook her head. "No," she said. "I'm letting you go." Her eyes snapped to the window, the lightning-slashed night's sky just as perilous as before. She then looked to Aveline again, her bracelets jangling like bones against cages, her breaths heavier than wind. "I'll calm the storms enough for you to flee the castle, into the streets.

Run. Run until you can fly. It's safer on the ground."

"What? Why? What's going—"

"It's—my parents, they're—" Thalissa gave a violent sigh, hands jerking. "That doesn't matter. I just cannot do this anymore."

"Can't do what?"

"I can't—I can't listen to you anymore! I can't listen to you pray and hope and love and—" Thalissa took a shuddering breath. "You remind me too much of—of—" Her voice cracked like glass underfoot. "I can't do this anymore. I can't take what has been taken from me. And—"

"And what?"

"And it doesn't fucking matter." Thalissa grabbed her by the shoulders, shaking her. "I don't want this anymore. Is that not what you wish me to say? You don't want to be here, either. And my parents are coming soon. If they see you, I cannot take this back."

Aveline stared, hardly able to breathe.

Had she been dropped into a dream? A nightmare?

"Go!" Thalissa demanded. "Now. Fuck—fucking *now*."

Aveline shuddered, gasping for breath like a fish amongst stars. Thalissa grabbed her by the waist, lifting her from the bed – hardly a challenge, given how she weighed almost nothing, but enough to make Aveline's whole body flush. A shard of glass dug into her foot as she landed on the floor, but she could hardly focus on that.

The wind that spiralled around the two of them made Thalissa's hair dance, the moonlight peeking through thunderclouds making her eyes shimmer. Something lay in her mind that could not spill through her lips; that much was obvious. But Thalissa's secrets hardly mattered.

Aveline's fists curled, her belly curdling.

"You're a monster."

Thalissa recoiled as if she had been slapped.

Aveline stepped forward.

Another shard embedded itself in her foot, but she paid no heed. Her screaming heart smothered every other sensation.

"You're going to ruin your kingdom," Aveline spat. "You are unfit to be queen. Even if you destroy your enemies, you are going to destroy yourself and your people in the process."

First, Thalissa's eyes were wide and startled. And then they narrowed into a fury that rivalled her captive's. "Excuse me?"

Aveline stepped forward again. "You don't care about your kingdom. You only care for your power. You did not steal me for your people, and, though I despise Styrme with every inch of my being, it deserves a queen who puts them first over everything. First over war, first over power, first over knowledge, first over freedom—"

As if a knife had impaled her heart, Aveline jolted. The words turned over in her mind, and something sour settled on her tongue.

She was not only yelling at Thalissa.

Why did Aveline wish to be queen?

Because she had to be. Because she had been raised to be. Because she had only ever wished to be free. Because. Because. Because!

But did Aveline really have no other choice?

Thalissa's lips twisted into a snarl. "I could kill you."

Aveline squared her shoulders. "You could. But you won't."

With a rough, bloodied hand, Thalissa grabbed Aveline by the front of her dress, yanking her closer so they were nose-to-nose. Her breath reeked of copper and storm.

Aveline did not bat an eye. "Kill me," she said. "Kill me, and ruin both our kingdoms beyond repair. Kill yourself in the process."

Thalissa breathed like she was drowning.

"Kill me," Aveline repeated, growing harsher and louder with every word. "Kill me! Do it, Thalissa, kill me! Fucking *kill me*!"

Thalissa dropped her.

Aveline landed in a puddle of raindrops and glass, but she did not allow herself to remain seated for long. She gathered several shards, slicing her fingers to ribbons, but did not drop them.

She leapt to her feet, and threw them each at Thalissa. Half of them bounced off her freshly-donned armour, as harmless as flies, but a few hit her face, slicing her dark, bruised cheeks. Blood trickled like tears.

"Kill me!" Aveline screamed. "Do it! Kill me!"

Thalissa surged forward, grabbing her by the front of her dress once again. "Run, little princess," she hissed. "Run for the sake of your kingdom and run for the sake of your people."

Every breath was yanked from Aveline's throat.

A moment passed. Two. Three.

Thalissa chuckled, shaking with bitter amusement. "You'll be no better a queen than I will. You know that, do you not?"

Aveline stared.

Aveline bit her tongue.

Aveline refused to look away.

"I wish never to lay eyes on you again," she said.

Something strange flashed in Thalissa's gaze, lightning against a dark night. Then, she dropped her, though Aveline did not again fall.

"We'll see." Thalissa shook her head. "Fly free, little dove."

As if Thalissa could control her every move, Aveline's wings unfurled, trembling and drenched. She turned, eyes on the window.

Behind her, Thalissa took a single breath, and the rustles and clinks indicated she was raising her bejewelled arms to the sky.

The glowering storm-clouds froze in place. Lightning became still cracks in the air. The rain hovered like crystals in the sky.

For a moment, the wind stopped, too, as if the kingdom of Styrme had forgotten how to breathe. Then, something golden twinkled in the corner of her gaze: sunbeams bursting through the night's sky. The wind resumed and grew tenfold. It plucked Aveline from the tower, though part of that came from her own will, and tossed her through the jagged maw that had once been the window.

Aveline was carried by the wind before her wings burst to life, before she began to really, truly fly. She soared through the air like a dove between tree-limbs, like her swans along the surface of her pond: free from troubles, free from strife.

Free from pain. Free from war.

Her foot wept crimson. The war continued.

But neither felt to be the case. Not in that moment.

She simply *flew*.

The wind cradled her with nothing less than desperate joy. It tickled her neck, almost retying her tangled mess of hair, though that was impossible. Impossible, but *something* held Aveline as she soared below the frozen clouds, over pointed turrets and rain-smeared roofs.

The castle was so enchanting that she was almost regretful of the missing chance to explore it.

It was oh-so different from her home, from her palace, from the entirety of her kingdom of Awin. It did not reside high above the ground, amongst the clouds, nestled in trees that would never die. It was low and dark, bricks crumbling, but strangely hypnotising.

Aveline could explore the lands of Ungode for an eternity.

Her gaze tilted upwards at the patches of stars overhead: the wing-like constellation that stretched from the shoulders of the earth, the white dots that formed still lightning, the patch of the Dark where the moon had once been. A beauty formed by the gods.

Aveline's heart settled in her throat, pounding so loudly that, as her feet hit the city streets, she could hear nothing but it and the wind.

They sang.

A few people snapped to look at her, like a golden-eyed girl having fallen to her knees; a raven with a white crown; a grey-haired man with a baby under his arm; and a gaggle of blueish children who cowered from the ragged, obvious enemy.

But Aveline had no time for them. Instead, she took a glance at the stars once again – barely visible, especially as the storms resumed with a violent snap – and determined exactly where north was.

Home.

How did she know this? Who was guiding her heart?

She ran as fast as she could, saving her wings' energy for when she really needed it. And, as she did so, she whispered.

Prayers. Wishes. Pleas.

Messages to her goddess.

She had helped Aveline once, during her attempt

to escape. And she had likely helped again. The wind supporting her flight over the castle could not have been entirely mundane, entirely *mortal*, even.

A breeze curled against her cheek.

Aveline's heart pounded, even more thunderous, and she spat her fears aside. Her determination settled in the murmuring cavern of her chest, and she quickened her pace.

Her feet hit the streets like the beating of rain, almost in time with the droplets themselves, just as vicious as they had seemed whilst nestled in her tower-turned-prison. Every sound brought her mind back to her captivity, even as she tried to focus on her escape.

Why had Thalissa released her?

What had prompted her change of heart?

Thalissa had let her go. Aveline was free.

She could ponder all she wished to, could pick apart the secrets kept, once she was back to her misty pond and dancing swans.

Aveline took a shuddering breath.

And she continued to race.

She sped through the streets. Her wings twitched with the itch to fly, even as the rain soaked them entirely, and *especially* as the wind screamed to pluck her from the ground and cradle her in its embrace.

Aveline reached the edge of the city, and found herself eye-to-eye with a range of looming mountains, capped with storms of every kind.

Some peaks were hidden by spiralling fog, some smothered with glistening snow, and many struck by bolts of lightning that never slowed. A constant, vicious attack.

Aveline's breaths stopped, as did her pounding steps, before the former resumed with a trembling uncertainty. She cast a glance back over her shoulder, and found the edges of this city had fewer people, but each stared right at her.

She was an obvious Awinian, though they would never know *who* she was. A spy, perhaps? None would make the right assumption.

An armour-clad figure emerged from a house of dark, crumbling brick, dragged by a fearful spouse and their teenage son. Though their face was hidden by an expressionless helmet, it was obvious what they were thinking, as if the wind carried it from their skull to her own.

Aveline was someone to capture.

In an instant, before her mind could catch up with her body's instincts, she shot upwards. The wind guided her with firm hands, and she dodged every crackle of lightning as they struck, leaving golden stains on the air, though each faded within moments.

Aveline could not focus on them, though they never once hit her.

She simply flew.

Over the shortest mountain, through the fog that coated its dark peak, and further and further and further until, finally, water came into sight.

Black. It churned like poison in a cauldron, though its salty aroma screamed nothing short of *freedom.*

Aveline had no idea how long she could continue to fly before she landed in the sea that would end her, infested with beasts aplenty. But she had to try. And she had *divinity* on her side.

The hand of her goddess was guiding her, keeping her steady, keeping her from losing the will to fly, even as her wings screamed. Aveline passed over ships and flashes of scaled beings dancing between the waves. Navy. Sapphire. Indigo.

A ship with sails of shimmering gold, heading in the very same direction. A dragon with amber wings, soaring east. A figure, nestled in one of the storm-clouds that grew sparser and weaker the further Aveline got from Styrme.

Her wings wailed, her limbs losing their last morsels of strength, but as she caught sight of the broken, floating islands of Alyro, to Awin's west, she knew she was close.

How had she flown so fast, when this should have taken days and days and days? *Had* this taken days? Though she had been right under the sky, she could hardly recall the brightening and darkening.

Why had her goddess lent a hand?

Aveline had no time for such questions.

Her eyes fixed on a tree taller than Styrmish mountains – with leaves of emerald and jade – and Aveline was filled with relief. But that relief soon turned to panic, as the grip of her goddess finally let go.

And Aveline was only as strong as her body allowed her to be.

She inhaled. She exhaled.

She fell.

Not to the ground, though she suspected that was mere luck, but into a branch that scraped her frail body. It caught her like a cage, its limbs wrapping around her torso as if the wind had grasped it and forced it to move. The breeze of an Awinian.

Her eyes lay their gaze on a figure emerging from the tiniest of sky-huts. A blue-black braid and skin like aged liquor. They grasped her by the shoulder, eyes wide and concerned as they recognised their princess.

For a moment, Aveline felt nothing but relief.

And then, once more, her vision was stolen away.

❋ ❋ ❋

"Aveline?"

Aveline could not open her eyes.

Her eyelids fluttered, but that was the most she could manage, her mind drifting in and out of consciousness, like a ship that had yet to decide whether to sail or drown. It did not listen to the screams of its sailors, but nor did her body listen to her wailing skull.

Hands caressed her face.

Gentle. Soft.

The same two hands every time, though others brushed her limbs and body and hands. Others combed her hair, ran fingers over scratches and scars, and tested her blood for impurities: for storm-sicknesses, curses, or poison. If she was contagious, she would never be touched again.

Aveline could hardly focus on them. She could hardly focus on anything more than the wind in her head, her heart, her lungs.

Visions danced across her eyelids. A gift.

A giver unknown.

Strangely, the first thing she *did* notice was her clothes. They were not the ragged scraps of the dress she had been stolen in, but the nightgown she had worn for years – almost every night, when she could get away with it – though her mother openly disapproved of her ownership of something so worn.

It was light, cool, and thin.

But the air around her was far from the terrible chill of her prison. It was… home. Home.

Aveline's mind snapped back to clarity, and her eyes flew open as she sat up, gasping for breath. Her hands curled into fists, filled with the bunched-up fabric of her nightgown. Her vision blurred. Her breaths quickened. Her organs ached. Nausea filled her from head to toe.

"Hey! Swan. *Swan.* It's okay. You're home. You're safe."

That voice... was that...?

Aveline locked eyes with Adonis. He was there, with his star-speckled irises and mess of curls and gaze that almost never left her face. And, following moments of wide-eyed relief, she began to weep.

Adonis's lightning-scarred face crumpled, and he threw his arms around her, pulling her in close and allowing her to rest her forehead against his shirt: thin and worn. Not armour.

His heart pounded steadily.

"You're home," he whispered, voice cracking. "You're home."

He allowed her to cry for far longer than anyone else would have.

Her parents. Her tutors. Her ladies. They had all grown sick of such weaknesses. They had all grown impatient with the delicate mind of a princess who had never known true hardship. Not until her taking.

Aveline's tears only overwhelmed her more fervently, more passionately, almost *violently*.

Adonis was *alive*.

He was riddled with scars, his every word emerging like his throat itched and his lungs ached. His body shook like even just *standing* exhausted him. And he, too, wept. But he was alive.

Had Thalissa truly shown him mercy, like she had – strangely – shown Aveline? Why? What did that mean?

Aveline supposed there was no way to know. She would never see Thalissa again. She would never get to spit curses or beg for answers from her. She would never again see those piercing eyes, never again hear the soft, thunderous voice.

Aveline lost her strength, collapsing out of bed, but Adonis caught her with ease. She never wished to part with him again.

She did not care what her parents said. She did not care what her parents did. She would stay in Adonis's arms until their hearts stopped beating, their skin slipped from their bones, and their bones crumbled into dust. And, even then, their souls would remain ever-intertwined.

Her people said life had begun in the kingdoms of the Air, though she did not know much of the story's truth. It had spread to the other elemental kingdoms next – those of Earth and Water, Fire and Metal and Ice, and, finally, Storms – and then into every other kingdom of the world: sixty-four in total. Forty-nine magics, each in sets of seven.

Life had begun in the Air, and there it would end, too, as the only moment Aveline would ever let go of Adonis would be when everything else was gone.

She squeezed him as tightly as she could.

Aveline suddenly knew what she had to do. She had escaped Styrme, unwedded and in one piece, and she was not trading one cage for another. Nothing mattered more.

But before Aveline could whisper anything – though her tongue would never spill the perfect song, not like she wished it to – the door opened, banging against the wall. With the fluttering of wings joining the trembling pair, Adonis pulled back.

Aveline squeaked, and did not allow Adonis to go far, gripping his sleeves with both hands. His breath hitched, his fingers slipping from her sides, though he did not step back.

Queen Aladie and King Barke came through.

Aveline caught a glimpse of their faces of despair, of concern, and then of relief. They crossed the room like hummingbirds, and Aveline was pulled from Adonis and into their arms.

She despised nothing more.

Barke pet her hair, and Aladie uttered the sweetest words Aveline had ever heard from her mother's lips. Nothing could compare, but she could hardly understand each honeyed affection and gratitude.

It could not possibly have been real.

They would never do or say these things, not in any other circumstance. And Aveline was startled by the fact that they were doing so now. But this was no dream.

Aveline held them in return.

Tears dripped down her face, though her sobs did not reach those smothered in Adonis's shoulder. And Aveline could think of nothing but him, him, him.

She cast her gaze through the gap between her mother and her father, and locked eyes with Adonis. He watched with something akin to despair, painted over his features and taking the sparkle from those dark, beautiful eyes. But he was himself. And he was alive.

Aveline yearned to hold him again. She would shatter her ribcage if it meant she could set her heart free.

He *lived*. That was everything she had hoped for, and nothing in all of Ungode mattered more. He lived, and he was there, right in her line of sight, so close, yet just out of reach.

That would change.

Aladie pulled back, Barke following suit, and she patted her daughter's pale, haggard face, though her own was far from dissimilar.

"Who took you?"

Aveline jolted, startled, and again locked gazes with Adonis. He knew who had taken her. He had *been* there.

Adonis had been there. He had tried his best to save her. He had done everything in his power to rescue her. Aveline knew that. And he had held her oh-so tightly upon her return.

Had he lied?

As if reading Aveline's mind, Adonis's expression crumbled like sand. "I don't remember." His voice broke. "I don't—there was nothing I could do to help, to find you. I don't remember anything after we arrived at your pond." His hand rose, tracing the strange, branching scars of a lightning strike. "I only remember the pain."

"We know it was someone of Styrme," Aladie spoke, her voice smoothing into something slower, more careful. "No one else could wield such power. And we suspect they had some potion to scramble your guardian's mind. We did everything we could to discover what he knew, and he was truthful. He remembers nothing."

Aveline's mouth dried. Her heart stuttered.

She could hardly speak, could hardly think.

"What did you do to Adonis?"

Aladie pet her daughter's well-combed hair. "He is unharmed, Aveline. We fixed him. You know of our healers of Blood and Flesh. We could have killed him for failing you so deeply, but we did not. We know of your fondness for him."

Fondness.

"You—you—"

Aladie cradled her cheek. "If he had anything to do with your taking, you must tell us now. He will be dealt with, along with whichever Styrmish criminal stole you from us."

Had they discovered Adonis's secrets, too? Aveline knew not what they were, but the thought alone had her bones quivering.

She searched for the right words for almost a minute.

The misty walls made her eyes ache, the cloudy scent making her chest tighten. The passing of time seemed unreal, like thinking through warped glass, especially after an arduous journey across the sea.

She shook her head.

"Adonis did everything in his power to save me," she whispered. "I remember it. But—but the Styrmish pirates were too strong."

Her tongue outpaced her mind, though she had no idea what she was doing, why she was spilling such falsehoods. A misplaced loyalty to the one who had, for reasons unknown, set her free?

Did Thalissa deserve that?

"Pirates?" Aladie prompted.

"I don't remember much, either," Aveline babbled. "My—my captors affected my memory, too. They—I remember nothing of them."

Thalissa had set her free. And Aveline would never be caged again.

She refused to be a pawn, not for either side.

"Of course," Aladie said, as smooth as ever and as saccharine as never. "We shall find your captors, and, I assure you, King Aliksone and Queen Flishe Gracetorn will punish them suitably. An execution, I believe." She shuddered, utterly ingenuine. "They have some barbaric practises in Styrme, but we shall have to adjust to them."

The air froze.

Aveline could not move, could not breathe. "What?"

Aladie gave her daughter a look of sympathy, fingers light against Aveline's tear-stained, once-bruised cheek. Finally, she smiled. "We have found you a suitable bride, Aveline. Awin and Styrme shall be united after generations of strife. I'm sure you'll adjust to the Styrmish climate, and I even ensured your knight shall be taken with you! Is that not all you ever could have imagined?"

Aveline could not respond.

"Aveline?" Adonis's voice cracked.

Aladie shot him a glare that had his next words dying. He cowered like never before, and that, more than anything, made Aveline tremble.

"What's the name of my bride-to-be, mother?"

She already knew the answer.

Aladie smiled, pleased, as if she lacked an inkling of Aveline's turmoil, though it was scribbled all over her face. "These preparations have been in the works for months," she said. "Of course, we never told you, or her, as only those in absolute power must be aware of these things. Styrme has a history, you see. Our people – our nobles, even – will object, though our kingdoms aligned will be unstoppable. We must set this in stone before anyone can get in the way."

Aveline swallowed. "The name, mother?"

Aladie gave her daughter a considering look, and then smiled once more. "Thalissa," she said. "Princess Thalissa Gracetorn."

* * *

Aveline could no longer slumber without the violence of storms accompanying her, without the cradle of fear, without the amber of flickering candlelight. Her bedroom was far too warm, encircling an ever-burning fireplace, lacking the chill of rainfall and wind.

Perhaps it was simply her racing mind, her overactive imagination, but she had never before felt so in danger: so at risk of eternal imprisonment. She gnawed on her lip and drew blood.

She had run out of tears to shed.

And she was alone. Alone, and in a too-big bed.

Alone, but not entirely. Adonis guarded her bedroom from the outside, as still and armed as metal-clad marble, though she had no idea when he had last slept.

They had hardly had a moment to talk.

And yet, they had communicated almost perfectly.

They both knew what they had to do. And though Adonis had hesitated like never before, it was clear he knew exactly how to get them out. And that he was willing.

But Aveline could hardly look him in the eye.

Not until the plan was finalised. Not until they were free.

Aveline pushed her blankets from her body, sitting up so suddenly it made her skull throb. She did not allow herself to dwell on the pain, however, and, instead, did something she had never done before. She left for her pond without alerting another.

Her window was strangely easy to break.

The flight made her worn wings wail, but she

ignored that. She simply flew, and soon landed on a now-charred branch. Her bare legs folded underneath her, and her skin prickled from the chill.

Though Aveline's thoughts were scrambled, she knew she had to do this *now*. Before she lay eyes on Thalissa again. Before she returned to that cage of a tower. Before an escape became an impossibility.

The only reassurance was that Thalissa had not known a thing.

Thalissa had no more power than Aveline did.

They each had those to follow without question. They each had only two choices: to obey those *really* in power, or to refuse. And if they refused, especially if they truly rebelled, they would never be seen again. They would die by a blade, or they would flee to where they could never be followed.

Aveline was almost certain of what Thalissa's choice had been, though she did not know of the outcome.

Thalissa had cast Aveline aside and allowed her to flee: a betrayal of the kingdom she had been raised to rule. But would she revoke the choice and steal Aveline once again? Would she give in to power?

Aveline did not know. She did not wish to guess.

But, she supposed, Thalissa's choice did not matter.

Aveline was going to take Adonis, and she was going to *escape*, using whatever secrets he had tucked up his sleeves, whatever allies she knew nothing about. They would flee to another set of kingdoms – not those of the elements, where she would be too-easily found, but to those further east: perhaps Palora of Plants.

That seemed far safer, far more easily hidden in. The largest of kingdoms, after all, filled with forests from border to border.

It would have trees to build homes in. It would have meadows to fly through, earth to touch. It would have shadows to dance amongst, night skies to gaze into, as a pair – hand-in-hand – drifted to sleep.

That was Aveline's only option.

If she wished for the freedom she had now caught a glimpse of, she would have to follow her heart. She had never done so before, but it was not too late to try.

She hoped.

Aveline stood, the charred branch's bark scraping her feet, making black flecks flutter through the air. She hardly watched the water now empty of swans, reflecting her lantern's light and sparkling like a night set with stars. She had no space in her heart for any of them anymore.

Aveline turned, ready to return to the bedroom Adonis protected from just outside: right within her grasp.

She took a breath. Her spine straightened.

And a golden hand slammed over her eyes, whilst another grabbed the back of her throat.

A CLAW
THROUGH
THE HEART

CHRYSANTHEMU M CLAWE

"Is that all you've got, Lucah?"

Clash. Dodge.

"The great follower of Blood. The fearsome pirate."

Block. Clash.

"Are you more of a weakling, a *fool* than the rumours suggest? If you cannot battle me – hardly trying at all – who are you to follow a captain such as yours?" She leapt over the low sweep of his blade.

Their swords moved with the speed of cracked whips, dancing with an elegance only seen on ballroom floors, and sang with a melodious tune, like the ringing of a bell. A merry laugh filled her throat, bubbling as if undersea, but was cut off by her enemy's scoff.

"Of course," he said. "You do not get to be the first mate of a ship like this without a skill like mine."

Clash. Block. Clash.

The sunlight danced over Chrysanthemum's

blade, transforming an ancient sword into naught more than a mirror. As it sliced and slashed and parried, it reflected her dark face and darker curls, and those feline eyes like marigolds and pollen.

"Oh, I don't know. Perhaps your captain has no sense. He could have promoted you for your skills in the bedroom, or perhaps even your looks alone." Chrysanthemum grinned over crossed blades – her teeth almost fanglike, though nothing compared to Lucah's. "Not that I would agree with that sentiment."

Block. Clash. Block.

Lucah's eyes were the richest of rubies and wine, especially as they narrowed in fury: a snap that came from so little, especially on the face of someone seldom uncomposed. He snarled like a violent beast, like he was made to *bite.* And yet, Chrysanthemum did not fear him.

She could never fear someone like him.

"My captain is the greatest man to ever grace this living sea: all seven great seas, in fact. Our ship would not rule the waves quite so fiercely had we not had our great Captain Dackon to lead us."

His sword thrusted forward, quick and forceful, like he wished to impale her entirely.

Chrysanthemum's lips quirked.

She dodged, light on her feet, despite her heavy boots, and the violent lunge missed her by inches. She grabbed him by the wrist, twisting as hard as she could, and the sword slipped from his grip. It hit the deck between a frayed rope and a splatter of dried copper.

With a metal-toed kick to his side, Lucah fell to the deck, knocking his head. He groaned. And as Chrysanthemum loomed over him, he rolled onto his back, sat up, and shot her a venomous glare. Hatred.

She almost believed it.

Chrysanthemum laughed and held out her hand.

Lucah stared, gave a serpentine hiss through clenched teeth, and then allowed her to pull him to his feet. His glove – a smooth, unstained white – was as cool as a night beneath stars.

He released her hand once he straightened, and then ran both of his own down his clothes: crimson and pearl, though without even a single splatter of blood. A long braid of spider-night hung down his back, wrapped in ivory webs. Jangling bracelets decorated both forearms, like veins bitten by metal and dripping with blood.

Though he looked prim and proper, he reeked of sea-salt and iron.

On his finger was a single gold ring: often indicative of marriage, of souls intertwined, but Lucah did not hold such a bond. That was known by all, and especially by those on board The Crimson Dead.

Chrysanthemum lifted her gaze from it, and gave him a crooked grin.

He did not immediately respond, but his face soon smoothed over: from the vicious fury of before to the cool elegance he usually expressed. Then, he looked over Chrysanthemum – just the simplest up-and-down of his eyes – before sending her a calmer stare.

"You fight well, Chrysanthemum. Who taught you?"

"I did," she responded, sheathing her sword and offering him a look of amusement. "You?"

Lucah adjusted his waistcoat. "My captain."

Chrysanthemum hummed, quiet, and cast a glance over her shoulder at the ever-locked door to the captain's cabin. She had yet to see what lay beyond, had hardly wished to, but everyone in the seven islands she journeyed between knew exactly what the captain of The Crimson Dead looked like. Followers seldom appeared as inhuman as he did.

A precious rarity. A *powerful* rarity.

And yet, an irrelevant one. He cared not for the hero who so often journeyed on his vessel, looking for quests in every corner of the Flesh.

Chrysanthemum turned back to Lucah, who watched her carefully, his face holding nothing but cool calculation. She had seen that expression every time she had boarded that ship. She did not particularly care what it meant.

Shifting her weight from one foot to the other, Chrysanthemum gave him a smile. "Are you looking for weaknesses, Lucah?"

Lucah sniffed, crossing his arms. "I don't need to. Do I?"

Chrysanthemum gave a bark of laughter,

throwing her head back as if what he had said was of utmost hilarity. As she did so, her eyes flicked over the sky, catching a glimpse of the birds and winged beasts that circled overhead. Yellow feathers. Brown fur. Green claws.

Their whistling languages sat on the tip of her tongue, but now was not the time for conversing with such creatures. Now was not the time for worshipping her god of Beasts.

She looked to Lucah once more, and he rolled his eyes. "My captain could destroy you in any fight, either way."

Chrysanthemum clapped him on the shoulder. "And yet he never has."

"He has had no need to." Lucah watched her warily, as if searching for the knowledge his magic of Blood would never grant him. "Though I suppose he should at least observe you. Heroes seldom do more than clash with pirates."

"You don't trust your captain's judgement?"

"Of course I do. But that does not mean I cannot be careful."

"I pick my battles."

"And is this one of them?"

"You'd know if it was."

Though his eyes remained cautious, Lucah nodded. "Understood."

Chrysanthemum gave a far grander nod in return, pocketing her hands in her skirt. It was just as torn as her shirt, as worn as the armour she often donned, but only enough that she found it charming and unique, rather than indicative of a violent life.

Her life was relatively violent. Heroism brought battles great and small. But she tried not to give off that impression with strangers.

It helped when she journeyed with pirates, however, even as their actions and beliefs misaligned. They were cheap, allowing passengers they deemed suitable entertainment, and rarely asked the kinds of questions she avoided answering. They were easy to amuse.

Chrysanthemum scanned the deck, finding dozens of pirates scattered all around, most of whom she had never spoken with. A boisterous group, filled with those who took great joy in the actions she found most despicable. They tormented each other with blades across skin, spewing blood as they cackled over conquests.

But *these* pirates seldom took the prisoners Chrysanthemum had freed from other ships. The Sapphire's Mercy. The Fury of the Drowned. The Red Witch.

The Crimson Dead made for fitting transportation. They brought her to the kinds of trouble she wished to fix.

As Chrysanthemum surveyed her surroundings, her eyes caught on something just beyond the ship – beyond its poppy-blood sails, its weapons impaled in the mast, its inebriated pirates slumbering across the deck – and her spine straightened.

Land.

Finally.

Chrysanthemum took a breath, and wandered as close to the front of the ship as she could, finding a stray stool to sit on, right in the eye of the sea. She spared a glance at the unconscious woman sprawled across the table and found her, thankfully, to be breathing. And unharmed.

Chrysanthemum turned forward, crossed one leg over the other, and watched. The ship cut through the water at a speed unmatched. Even its figurehead of a half-skeletal corpse made no difference to how it sliced the sea. A sharpened knife through fresh flesh.

The thought made Chrysanthemum shiver, but she knew not to make her disgust known amongst *these* kinds of people.

Entertaining, occasionally. She could give them that.

But a hero would, one day, destroy them.

And they would have earned it.

Of course, she would never be that hero. But Chrysanthemum was one of many. Someone would fulfil the quest she had no heart to take.

Someone always did.

She swallowed the lump in her throat and continued to watch the land approach: a sliver, at first, but it bloomed like a flower.

Chrysanthemum could almost *taste* the growls and the hisses of beasts looking only for companionship. The forests of Beake were full of them: more souls than trees, more hearts than roots.

And they adored the ones who understood them, unlike almost every other being in Ungode, even in the kingdom they called home.

A welcome relief, after her last quest.

Chrysanthemum was so distracted by the thought of little lives – little *beasts* – to chatter with, that she was ignorant of someone taking a seat behind her, pushing the slumbering woman aside. She only noticed as a deep, thick voice cleared its throat.

Her hand flew to her sword's handle and she spun in her seat.

The man across from her was as towering as an oak and even more muscular than Chrysanthemum was. His skin was the white of bone, scattered with shimmering scars of every shape and size. His long hair was like a waterfall of blood, as if dripping from a long, thin cut. And his eyes were that same shade of solid crimson. He did not blink, and was dressed in clothes that bordered on royalty.

Deep reds. Pure whites. Flecks of gold.

Captain Dackon raised an eyebrow at Chrysanthemum, especially as she stared like she had seen nothing stranger. He was a follower like no other, though half of that came from aura alone, as if something spilled from his pores and spiralled in the air around him. Power.

"Chrysanthemum."

"Yes…?" Chrysanthemum's hand perched on her hilt.

Dackon's spider-web sword was almost a thing of legend, even more ancient than the kingdoms they journeyed between. But his sheath was missing from his belt. If it came down to a fight, she would win.

Chrysanthemum had heard the rumours that perhaps should have made her take pause. But she knew not of their veracity.

Dackon watched for a moment longer.

Or, at least, he *seemed* to watch. His eyes were immovable, unblinking, and so solid they were impossible to track.

He placed one hand on the table, folding the other on top. They were decorated with rings of ruby-gold, on all fingers but the one indicative of marriage. "You're looking for your next quest, are you not?"

Chrysanthemum nodded. Slow. "Yes, I am."

"Then I have information you may wish to know." Dackon gave a pause. "Perhaps not information, per se. But guidance."

He did not elaborate.

Instead, Chrysanthemum was left to watch in bewilderment and caution, until the words in her mind finally reached her lips, laced with something wary. "What is your guidance… captain?"

"You are not to call me that."

Chrysanthemum shivered like a spider had

scuttled up her spine, but nodded. A thought then struck her like lightning.

Who was she to cower?

She could take any pirate in a fight. Any pirate who deserved it.

Her spine straightened, the grip on her sword tightening. She gave the cool-faced Dackon a look that embodied her growing courage and nothing more. She placed her other hand on the table, and began to drum a soft, rhythmic tune, like the beating of a heart.

Dackon stared for a moment longer, before he leant in, smelling of old books and blood. "Don't stay in Beake for long."

Chrysanthemum blinked. "Excuse me?"

"Don't stay in Beake for long."

"No, I heard you—"

"I have ways of foreseeing," Dackon interrupted. "I may be of Blood, but I have allies, family, followers of every kind. I know much. And I know my Lucah is somewhat fond of you. There are things in Beake that mean to do you harm. You may not return in one piece."

Chrysanthemum stared.

Suspicion swirled with the bewilderment and dread in her gut.

How was she to trust a man like him? She knew of the blood he spilled. She had breathed the stench of copper, splattered across the deck of his ship. Some stains looked to have been there for longer than its crew – and its captain – could have lived.

A stolen vessel, of course. One never not used for violence.

And Dackon was a pirate. A breed of villain known for their uncalculated chaos. An intelligent one – one with powers far beyond one beast-speaking follower – but a pirate nonetheless.

Chrysanthemum knew villains. She knew which she could trust.

Her jaw tensed, boot hitting the deck with calculating taps. She did not allow her distrust to sit so obviously in her eyes, though she was, of course, unable to tell what Dackon did and did not believe.

But that was not her problem.

"There is nothing more to tell you." Dackon stood. "I have done my duty. I have done what I must to ensure my pet remains satisfied."

Chrysanthemum's sword-hand twitched.

"Enjoy your stay in Beake, little hero," Dackon said, waving dismissively. "I hope to see you again, and not as a corpse to be feasted upon." As he began to walk away, he did not look back over his shoulder, but his continued words could not have been more obviously tossed at her. "Good luck."

Chrysanthemum stared, hands in fists, as Dackon wandered through the parting crowd. He settled in front of Lucah, catching him by the shoulder, and Lucah's face morphed into one of pure bliss.

She sighed. Her eyes closed.

Her hand lifted from her sword, pinching the bridge of her nose.

Lucah was interesting, she supposed, if a little pathetic.

But she could not wait to leave this ship.

* * *

Chrysanthemum's boots pounded against the uneven dirt path, weaving around bushes and over fallen, moss-covered logs. In the back of her mind, she wondered how carriages and wagons navigated the endless twists and turns, but that was far from her focus.

"A follower!"

Chrysanthemum chuckled, raising her hand to the pinkish bird that fluttered overhead, feathers like the fluff of a lion's mane. She waved, and let out a low, sharp whistle. It made a twittering, delighted sound – the only laughter a creature like that could make – and, soon it was joined by others: equally wild and delighted.

Birds in every shade. Feathers in cream, gold, green. Insects with sparkling wings. Reptiles that danced amongst patches of mist.

They should not have been so surprised to find one who understood their whistles and growls. But Beake had changed, at least since Chrysanthemum had been a child. Though it was an ancient kingdom, followers of all kinds were no longer so commonplace.

The southern forests were filled with the deadliest of beasts, though were not quite so perilous as the northern mountains: cavernous and splattered with blood in every shade. Those of Beake had grown wary, whether necessitated or not.

She drummed her fingers on her sword's hilt, and her tune morphed from a simple communication and into a merry melody, picked up from sailors over a decade ago. As the music's pace quickened, echoed by those who followed her, it grew into a cacophonous chorus.

Every creature sang along.

Chrysanthemum could hardly focus on her path, though she navigated the forest with an instinctual ease. Instead, her mind was filled with melodies and whisper-whisper-whispers.

The creatures of the forest had much to sing about.

She only noticed the ending of her path when the song of the beasts began to fade: voices slipping into the background, scaled deer ceasing to follow, feathered insects growing fearful and soft. They were, it seemed, too close to a human settlement.

A settlement not on Chrysanthemum's maps.

As the curling smoke of a brick chimney came into sight, Chrysanthemum found herself coming to a halt, as if she were just as unwelcome as those that lacked an intelligent mind. Her whistles ceased, and the remaining animals scurried or fluttered away, though a few birds remained in the nearest trees.

Watching. Whistling. Whispering.

Chrysanthemum tuned them out.

She glanced around, running her fingers over the grooves of her sword, before her resolve returned. She broke through the thick trees, ducking under a cobweb, and found a handful of small, sturdy buildings, though their roads led to more. They were dark, with reinforced windows and sturdy walls. Most looked to be houses, though no one lingered outside, but a few were obvious stores.

Right in front of Chrysanthemum, with that curling chimney-smoke, was a larger building with an engraved sign, indicating that this was the tavern. She paused, glancing around, before her gaze focused on it. The windows were barred, the door thick, but candlelight was visible through the cleaner parts of glass. This place was unabandoned.

For a moment, Chrysanthemum hovered in indecision, warnings and hesitations drifting through her ears. But she was no coward.

If she wished for information, for any quest a follower of Beasts was suitable to take, that was where she would find it. In every village, town, and city, no matter the kingdom, a tavern served the loose-tongued folk who would share anything weighing on their minds. Malice and plight.

And they, without exception, held the most

interesting of stories.

Chrysanthemum nodded, firm, and marched over to the door, pushing it open with a long, slow creak: the entrance of a stranger in any play. Every eye in the tavern landed on her. And there were *many* eyes, far more than such a simple village should have held, though dusk *was* approaching. The time for drinking had begun.

She smiled, raising a hand to wave at those who stared, though most returned to their meals and drinks within moments.

The aroma of roasted meat wafted through the air – accompanied by the stench of blood, though that was her heightened sense of smell – but Chrysanthemum ignored it, though it turned her stomach. Instead of wrinkling her nose, she marched over to the bar, taking an empty seat between a teenager sipping at rum, and a woman with black braids and one silver earring.

The woman cast her a glance, lingering on Chrysanthemum's sword, before she looked away, and took a long, slow sip from her mug. She had a thin, pretty frame and dark, hooded eyes, with a look to her face that whispered secrets aplenty.

Chrysanthemum turned to the tavernkeeper, who raised an eyebrow, before allowing her to order a drink. It came quickly, and she dropped a pair of coins into his hand: one blessed to make his hair shiny, the other to frighten away a certain breed of wasp, though both only worked when held in both palms, and only for him once. Cheap.

And once she had taken her first sip, she caught his eye once more.

Straightening in her seat, she lowered her mug, but he spoke before she could. "Are you looking for trouble, miss?"

Chrysanthemum laughed, jovial and sweet, and patted her sword like a pet. "I assure you; I mean well," she said. "This sword is for my protection alone, nothing more."

"My patrons are wary of more than your sword."

"Oh?" She smiled, leaning in and blinking rapidly, making the yellow of her eyes far brighter, especially against her cool skin. "Do you all have something against followers, sir?"

The woman beside her snorted. Their eyes locked – ink against honey – before the other woman smiled. She lowered her drink, outstretched her hand, and shook Chrysanthemum's with a firm grip.

"Heroes aren't exactly welcome around these parts," she said, smiling as if she were nothing of the sort. "And these folk are wary of any follower, either way."

Chrysanthemum chuckled, leaning back and crossing her arms against her chest. "Then I suppose *you* aren't one?"

"You're an observant one, aren't you? I'm far from it. Unless you consider humans to be followers of the Mundane, of course."

"I've heard whispers, but we aren't exactly the same thing."

The woman nodded, slow and amused, and took a sip of her own drink, leaving a blue stain on her lips. She gave Chrysanthemum a charming smile. "What's a hero doing here? Are you looking for your next adventure? Some quest to take, some damsel in distress?"

"As is the life of a hero."

The woman chuckled. "Well, you're not going to find much around here. These are quiet folk. That's why this is where I'm drinking, instead of somewhere with more... spark."

"You like a peaceful life?"

"Something like that."

Chrysanthemum laughed. "And where would I find my quest? I mean, I'm an obvious stranger to this part of Beake. I grew up in the west, not the south. I haven't been down here in years. I've spent the last decade in Palora, most of all."

"Clearly."

Another sip. A look of contemplation.

The woman drummed painted nails against her mug, before pulling away. She dug through the pockets of her night-dark coat, and retrieved a folded scrap of paper. She placed it on the bar, managing not to spill either drink, and smoothed it over with her palms.

A map. Beake.

"We're here," the woman said, tapping a southern corner, nestled right beside the sea, a forest alone between waves – speckled with sea-beasts – and the quiet little town. She slid her finger up. "Snikett is where you'll find something. It's a small city, even got a castle for the nobles. There'll be something there to catch your eye, trust me."

The woman then stood, jolting Chrysanthemum, who had leant in to examine the stained, creased paper: ancient, she assumed, though oddly accurate. As Chrysanthemum gave her a look of bewilderment, the woman reached for her drink, chugging the rest with one swig, before returning the mug to the barkeeper.

Chrysanthemum blinked, and then laughed. "Are you going somewhere, mysterious stranger?"

The woman laughed, too, fixing her braids. Her earring shimmered in the lantern-light, more gold than silver, at that angle. It cast a shadow on her cheek. "You're not the only one with quests to follow, pretty hero. My captain awaits me."

Chrysanthemum's eyebrows shot upwards. "Captain?"

Why did she always find the....

She looked to the map, a little taken aback, before her eyes fixed on the littlest letters in the bottom right corner: shimmering and curled.

A. Hom.

A name, perhaps?

Chrysanthemum turned back to her, lips parting to call after the woman who had forgotten her map. "Hey, you—"

She locked gazes with the wanted poster on the closing door, smeared beyond recognition with some strange, golden paint. Or perhaps that had once been the hair? It was unclear.

There was no longer any sign of the woman who had abandoned her map, giving Chrysanthemum the vague impression that she would be impossible to follow, though she had no idea why. After a moment, she shrugged, though the impression lingered in her mind, and turned back to her mug. She took a sip and spared another glance at the map.

At least now she knew where she was going, though it seemed a tad easy. But first she had to finish her drink.

* * *

Snikett.

Chrysanthemum had visited many cities, almost more than she could count. Cities ruled by magic or the mundane. Cities of violence and bloodshed, and cities never once knowing war. Cities one with nature, and cities without a living being in sight.

She had never seen a city like this before.

The buildings were short and bulbous, with high gates to keep out animals and thick windows that could never shatter. Animal skulls were planted on sticks, reeking of dead blood and akin to the warning flags on pirate masts. Plants speckled the paths like freckled flesh. Stalls sat on almost every street, though chests were padlocked. There was even a meadow with wooden spikes to clamber and play with.

And it was empty. Abandoned.

The streets held not a soul, though footprints of brown and red indicated it had emptied not long ago. The trapdoors on several streets led only to silent tunnels. There were even no people in the houses Chrysanthemum broke into.

And the closer she grew to the centre of the city – to the castle she knew would hold answers – it only worsened. Cobblestone streets had large, cracked pits. Walls, once invincible, crumbled. Toys lay abandoned, hastily dropped and never retrieved. Not in the chaos.

A shiver ran down Chrysanthemum's spine like the scuttling of an insect. What had happened here?

Her sword was unsheathed, her shield brandished, and she moved with slow, careful steps. She ducked behind walls whenever she heard a sound, clutching her weapons to her chest, though each noise, so far, had only been a fox or a hare or a deer. And those were few and far between. They each fled upon spotting her, even as she called to them in their own language.

That was what unsettled Chrysanthemum most.

At least, it was what unsettled her most... until she was struck by the snore. A deep, rumbling snore, rough and thunderous, the street trembling from the moment it was in earshot. It was deafening, almost, but could not be mistaken for anything else.

It came from a great, slumbering beast. That much was clear.

A great, slumbering beast, likely buried in the belly of the castle, as that was where she was headed, if the signs were to be believed. It could have claws the length of her torso, able to tear her in two. A mouth that would gobble her in one bite.

The crunching of bones echoed through her mind, so vivid it bordered on memory. Chrysanthemum lowered her sword.

She was not one to start a fight she could not finish. She had abandoned that habit half a decade ago, learning from prisons and plight. And she was as unprepared for this as one could get.

Her gaze fixed onto the clouded sky – empty of birds, feathered or furred – before it returned to the street behind her, dotted with debris. It lacked even *insects;* there was no one this close to the deafening snore. Every so often, she caught a flash of vibrant wings, a glimpse of a curling tail, but that could have been her imagination.

Whenever she spun, she found nothing.

Chrysanthemum stopped in place, and glanced back and forth between the path ahead and the path behind. Once. Twice. Thrice.

The street continued to shudder like an orphan afraid.

Which way to turn? Should she follow what echoed?

Her fingers squeezed her sword's hilt, and she made her decision.

The city was surrounded by forests, thick and pulsing, and animals great and small. Chrysanthemum would find *some* creature to assist her, no matter their species or size. She had a knack for it, even without taking her magic into account. They would tell her everything.

And Dackon's warning lingered in the back of her mind.

Chrysanthemum nodded to herself. Once she knew the species of the beast, she would take her next step.

She turned, steady and sure, and travelled back down the street, around cracked pits and shattered glass and stuffed dolls leaking cotton-blood. Her steps were light, despite her heavy leather-metal boots.

If she had not awoken the beast by heading in its direction, she would not awaken it as she fled.

She moved at a quickened pace until she reached the edge of the city: thick, towering trees filling her vision. Without hesitation, she crossed the pebbles separating stone from dirt, delving into the forest beyond.

The animals were sparse, hidden, and did not respond to her calls.

She knew they were there, just as they knew she was; she could hear their scurrying steps and hissing breaths. The buzzing of wings and the padding of paws and the whining of cubs.

But something had frightened them.

This beast was beyond them, too.

Chrysanthemum liked to think of herself as strong, determined, and fearless. She liked to think of herself as the hero no one had thought she could be. She knew what she was; she knew what she could do.

Maidens had gifted her roses upon rescue. Wolves had licked her cheeks like puppies. Pirates had laughed but released her from cages.

There were things she would never resort to, things she refused to even consider. Violence was never her first choice. But she could fight, and she could win. She *often* won.

Chrysanthemum simply had to follow her instincts.

She picked up the pace, boots like the stomp of an elephant, listening as the wails of predator and prey filled her skull. They sang warnings incomprehensible, like their minds had been scrambled.

In her presence, they gained an intelligence like her own. But something had terrified them past the point of comprehension. This was not entirely out of the ordinary, but it set Chrysanthemum on edge, though she did everything she could to calm her racing heart.

The scent of smoke hit her like a slap to the face.

She stumbled but did not lose her shield or sword. Her eyes widened, and she looked around, frantic, before realisation set in.

It was not the stench of a phoenix mid-battle. It smelt of... meat.

Chrysanthemum shuddered, but her shoulders slumped.

With the speed of a sloth, she followed that stench of smoke, though tried not to inhale too much, lest she lose the little food that remained in her belly: roots, berries, and stale bread. She curled around trees, trampled bushes and flowers, dodged beetles and snails, before, finally, something purple caught her eye.

A tent, made of the scaled, violet skin of some animal even Chrysanthemum could not identify. And, as she approached, she found more. Tents of various shades: some of skin, some of fur, some of woven fabric. There were about a dozen of them, hastily constructed. And, in the centre, there was a large campfire, with some pig-like creature roasting on a spit: face frozen in eternal agony.

Chrysanthemum flinched.

A handful of families, gathered on fallen logs, were in the midst of mournful conversation. Once one spotted Chrysanthemum, breaking through the trees, the rest did, too. They leapt to their feet in a panic. Most fled to the opposite corner of the campsite, whilst the rest drew weapons. They held themselves like they had never known battle.

Chrysanthemum sheathed her sword, but kept her shield locked onto her arm. "I mean no harm! Are you the people of Snikett?"

They whispered frantically amongst

themselves. Chrysanthemum caught snippets – they feared her sword, her stance, her *eyes* – but she was missing quite a bit of context. If they really were of Snikett, what had frightened them into fleeing?

A woman pushed through the crowd, which parted and reformed around her like water. Her skin was a light brown, her figure tall and rounded, and her face was speckled with violet freckles, matching the petal-like waves of her hair. She wore large, round glasses, and, upon closer inspection, her flowing dress was formed entirely of scales of lavender and cream. It looked like armour, but would do little in battle.

A follower?

She certainly had the appearance of one, but it was unclear which god she called her own.

She held herself like she did not know how to be a leader, her pretty face crinkled with worry, but the crowd looked to her as if she were the bravest of them all. Why did they not fear her beauty, when they feared Chrysanthemum's eyes most of all?

Shifting her weight from one foot to the other, Chrysanthemum offered a smile. "Chrysanthemum Clawe," she said. "And you are?"

The woman pursed her lips, looking her over, before she, too, smiled: gentle, though with lingering caution. Chrysanthemum liked her already, though perhaps it was simply those enrapturing eyes.

"Kaydah Latche," she said. "Perhaps we should talk in my tent?"

She gestured to the one of violet scales – the largest of all, closer to Snikett than the rest – and Chrysanthemum cast it a wary glance.

If need be, she would win the fight, even in such close quarters.

Chrysanthemum looked back to Kaydah, fixing a charming smile onto her face. "Of course!" She gestured grandly. "Lead the way."

Kaydah nodded, and crossed the clearing with quick, light steps, balancing on the balls of her feet. She passed Chrysanthemum, and led her into the tent. As soon as they were through the fabric door, they sat, each on a makeshift bed of blankets and clothes. The room lingered between cosy and cramped, but, after a moment's pondering, Chrysanthemum decided to consider it the former.

Kaydah settled in place, smoothing hands over her skirt. "You're a follower of Beasts, I presume?"

Chrysanthemum nodded, chuckling. "Did the eyes give it away?"

"I couldn't be certain, but you carry yourself like a blessed one."

"And you don't?"

"I'm not a follower."

Chrysanthemum blinked, a little surprised, taking in Kaydah's freckles and locks, like someone had gathered flowers and scattered petals across her skin. She gestured vaguely to the features, before realising that such an action might be considered impolite.

She bit her tongue before she could splutter something embarrassing.

Kaydah gave a little laugh. "I know what I look like, and I know the effect I often have." She folded one hand over the other in her lap. "My parents were of Disease, though my sister and I were raised in Beake, despite the conflicts. We share some of our mother's features, but my sister and I are completely mundane, I assure you."

Chrysanthemum leant back. "Huh. Well, you fooled me. I guess it may come in handy, if you ever need to frighten some foe."

"That's something I rarely partake in."

"Right. You don't seem the type." Chrysanthemum laughed. "Well, then I'm sorry if I offended you, Miss Latche."

Kaydah's lips twitched. "I took no offense."

"Good. Good."

They lapsed into silence, and Chrysanthemum's thoughts snapped back to where she was, what she was doing. Was this the best use of her time, to chatter with a pretty lady, when there was a beast to chase, to catch, to conquer? Those enrapturing eyes almost *were* a disease...

But if anyone was to know what had driven thousands from their home, it would be one of its citizens.

She and Kaydah locked gazes once more, and Chrysanthemum found herself overwhelmed by that beauty once again, as if it could swallow her whole. Was she simply too easily enraptured?

She shook away the thought.

Kaydah held a curious look. "What kind of follower are you?"

"What kind? Beasts?"

"No. That I understood."

"Then…?"

"We don't see many followers around here. I'm about as strange as you can get." She gestured vaguely with one hand, adjusting her glasses with the other. "Heroes and villains pass through, on occasion, but that's about it. Which are you?"

"You allowed me into your home without knowing which I am? Is that the safest thing to do, Miss Latche?"

Kaydah smothered a chuckle. "Perhaps not."

"I didn't realise southern Beake was so against us. Most kingdoms adore their followers." Chrysanthemum's eyes flicked over the scale-skin of the tent, before brushing over Kaydah's freckles. "I've learnt a lot in the last few days."

"Are you not a hero, nor a villain, then?"

"Oh, no. I'm a hero. I'd like to consider myself one, at least."

"You look like one."

"Then why'd you ask?"

"Oh, caution, I suppose. My neighbours would wish me to." Kaydah's whole body then tensed, as if some strange thought had suddenly overcome her. "You must be here for the beast."

There was a beat.

Chrysanthemum's heart settled into smooth neutrality, though remained somewhat unsettled by the new look in Kaydah's eyes. "So, it is a beast. I assumed as much, but you can never be too sure."

Kaydah's hands balled the bed's fabric into fists.

Chrysanthemum's tongue slid over her teeth.

Dackon's words echoed through her skull, though she tried to push the feeling aside. She focused on Kaydah's face instead, especially as it flickered like her true emotions were smothered.

Chrysanthemum waited.

Kaydah took a breath, before finally speaking, her voice barely above a whisper. "It overtook the castle first. Our nobles fled, leaving those in the dungeons to be eaten. It set our crops ablaze, chased away the animals tame enough to be kept in barns. And it spread. There are no safe places remaining in Snikett."

Had Chrysanthemum known her better, perhaps she would have attempted some sweet comfort. But she did not. Instead, her lips remained shut, hiding her pointed teeth, as she hoped her eyes were not too unsettling to one in such peril.

Kaydah continued. "Everyone fled. It was... chaos. I think most ran as far as they could – carriages destroyed by too many people wishing to use them – but some of us settled nearby." Her spine straightened, leaving her a little taller than Chrysanthemum. "I set up this campsite with my neighbours, and... I suppose they look to me, though I've never been more than a seamstress."

"You're stronger than you think," Chrysanthemum said, the words rolling easily from her tongue. "You're talking to me when no one else would. I think you deserve to be looked to."

As Kaydah blinked, her cheeks darkened. She tilted her head, looking her over. "You're a charmer, Miss Clawe."

Chrysanthemum grinned. "I try to be."

"Are you fearless, too?"

"I'd like to think so."

"And are you fearless enough to save my people?"

Chrysanthemum leant in, her gaze firm and steady.

She knew what she could do; she knew that with clarity. She knew of her strengths, her weaknesses. And she had fought many a beast in her day, more than she could count. It did not matter that she had yet to face a creature of this apparent magnitude, that she had yet to form the perfect plan. She could do this.

Her eyes fixed on Kaydah's. "I'm fearless enough to try."

Kaydah nodded, firm, in return. Her eyes sparkled with something akin to hope. "Good. We need someone like that." She paused, pensive, before frowning. "What did you see of the beast? Its tail, its claws?"

"I didn't get close enough. I heard the snoring

and figured I'd need a real plan. I won't be much use without one."

Kaydah's eyebrows rose. "You know not of its species?"

Chrysanthemum's brow furrowed, something uneasy spiking in her gut. Her eyes flitted to the door of the tent, but the shadows only indicated the presence of near trees, her ears catching nothing but the wind. It seemed the people still cowered as far as they could.

She ran her tongue over her teeth. "What is it?"

Kaydah shuddered. "Only the rarest, most dangerous of beasts."

Chrysanthemum had encountered many beasts: violent giants, far more perilous to fight than the average creature. They had often been granted such a title by those who had simply never seen worse. She had heard it all before. But something in Kaydah's voice left Chrysanthemum more than a little unsettled.

She leant in. "What is it?"

There was a pause. A thick, weighted pause.

"A dragon."

✳ ✳ ✳

The tail caught Chrysanthemum's eye first.

Long. Thick. Scaled. It sparkled like ambers aflame, ended with a pin-sharp spike, and protruded through a crumbling hole in the castle's wall, almost twice her height when she reached to the sky.

It was akin to a sunset, impossible to tear eyes from, echoing through the sky like a visual melody, written by the gods.

No, it was more a *sunrise.*

A beginning. A beauty and a horror yet to come.

Chrysanthemum shuddered, ducking behind the house she observed from. In its small alleyway lay her supplies: some provided by Kaydah, by the bravest of her neighbours, and the rest having either been scavenged or already sitting in her bag.

She tended to carry light.

As she crouched, she ran her fingers over various weapons, each polished until they shone.

Knives of Blodrik. Blood.

An axe with a living wooden handle. Palora of Plants.

Her ancient sword, not of any magic, but forged by a blacksmith in the mundane kingdom of Mundan – not to be looked down upon.

Chrysanthemum's hand stopped over a weapon she rarely used.

Her bow. And her quiver of arrows.

After a moment's contemplation, she plucked the bow from the ground, swinging the quiver over her shoulder, and turned back to the house that stood right between her and the beast.

The air simmered with heat.

Chrysanthemum had already shed as many layers as she could, even abandoning her armour, as that meant little against the teeth and claws of a dragon, let alone its breaths of bubbling flames. Still, her blood churned and boiled, as if she were perched in a campfire.

Her trepidations echoed through her skull – empty, for once, of the voices of creatures that so often chattered in her ears. They, too, feared the dragon, it seemed. For good reason.

A beast of multiple gods was not one to be ignored, to be looked down upon. Humans could never hope to hold such power.

Most were not strong enough for even one.

Beasts and Fire and Change.

Those were who the dragon worshipped.

It could have come from Beake, from Flaymer or Flik, from Chymae. There was no way to tell how ancient it may have been. There was no way to know how much blood had splattered its teeth and claws.

The godsland below was its only true home.

Its scales were bright and polished, but retained their memories of scarlet. Chrysanthemum could hardly imagine the terror it had wrought.

It would take a team of followers to tackle a dragon in ordinary circumstances, to pin those wings and slice it in two. But, it seemed, Chrysanthemum was the only one willing to try.

A city that chased away its magic chased away its heroes, too.

Her grip on her bow tightened, the grooves deep and tangible, even through her impenetrable gloves. She took a heavy breath, and then peered around the building for the dozenth time.

The tail had yet to move. And the thunderous, rumbling snores indicated the beast continued to slumber. The stone streets trembled as if fearful, and the fallen remains of crumbled bricks bounced and danced as if attempting to flee.

Dragons could slumber for weeks. Months. Years. But they were easily awoken, she believed, in the right circumstances.

A sudden attack was not a risk to take.

Chrysanthemum had survived long enough to know that. She had the scars to prove it from other beasts she had faced, the warped, clawed flesh across her chest and back often frightening the women who slipped into bed with her. Her fingers twitched at the memories.

Chrysanthemum could hardly think about that. It hardly mattered if a new scar joined her twisted collection.

Instead, she watched the tail as it jerked. What was the dragon dreaming of, what filled its slumbering mind? Did it think of fire and brimstone, or something softer, kinder?

The thought of killing such a beast, even knowing what it had done, made her heart ache. But she had done so before. And she could do so again, if the need arose. What choice did she have?

Chrysanthemum chewed her tongue, and began to take slow, careful steps towards the dragon. Her boots were as silent as could be, like the hops of a hare, though every movement boomed. With every snore that seemed too loud – or too quiet – she froze. A fawn in lantern-light.

She waited. The grumbling resumed. She did, too.

As she reached the end of its tail, she halted so quickly she almost tumbled. Her eyes fixed on an indent in the stone, large enough that she could lay in it – limbs splayed – and would not reach the edges with the tips of her fingers nor the tips of her toes.

A footprint. Gold.

Had it been left by the dragon? It had to have been.

A warning, almost. A warning to flee, but not one given by the dragon itself. It had not been given by *anyone*. This was simply Chrysanthemum's mind realising how utterly in danger she was.

Its foot alone could crush her.

She took a breath, and then spun back around. She had felled many a beast in her day. She had been a hero since she was *fifteen* – never halting, never stumbling, never looking back on what she had left behind – and she was more than double that now. She may not have fought a dragon, may not yet know what to do, but she was not helpless.

Chrysanthemum's resolution only grew.

Kaydah's face in her mind was inescapable. A reminder of who she had yet to save. A stranger, most of all, but Chrysanthemum had battled on the behalf of those whose faces she had never seen, on the behalf of nobody at all. A woman she had conversed with – albeit only once – was more than enough reason to fight.

Chrysanthemum quickened her pace as she returned to her alleyway and crouched beside her patchwork bag. She dug through it, pushing aside bottles, food wrapped in paper, and the bits of dirt she had never completely brushed away. Her fingers closed around leather.

A smile crossed her features, and she retrieved a book.

It had been so long since she last needed it. She had almost forgotten she still had it, buried under what was more-often used.

Chrysanthemum did not know who it had once belonged to; the gold name had been smudged since she had discovered it. But the ink across the pages, as yellow as her eyes, were as pristine as it always had been, since the day she had fetched it from the ashes of a library. And the illustrations were nothing but perfect.

She flicked through the pages.

Beasts of every size, every shape, every magic, flashing, flickering, twitching. Hypnotising, on occasion, but Chrysanthemum was only focused on one thing. A snarling dragon, painted in amber, covered the final page, spewing flames across the paper.

Her stomach churned. Her eyes darted over every word.

It holds a bulbous belly of fire and ash, fuelled by

the creatures it consumes. Its magic spews as flames through rows of bloodied teeth, reducing everything touched to nothing.

Its size changes to adapt to its surroundings. One moment, a horse-fly. The next, a palace.

Impenetrable scales.

Ancient. A body that never ages.

One weakness. Gullet.

Chrysanthemum sighed heavily. Her eyes closed. Her head knocked against the wall behind her. Shit.

A weakness was more than she could have hoped for. But a weakness like that was almost impossible to exploit. Would she have to fire an arrow down its throat? She could not hit it with her sword, not without crawling inside its mouth like a fool.

Could she risk that? Could she allow it to open its jaw, to brew fire behind its teeth, with less than a moment to shoot?

Chrysanthemum could flee. She could never return to this city, never look Kaydah in the eye, but her soul would never settle. She would never think of anything but the people she had failed to save.

It would *haunt* her.

Chrysanthemum took a breath, and then stood.

She needed more information. Dragons were a rarity, formed from the fallen jewels of the Beast-god's crown. Every creature was born from his ever-falling limbs. Snakes were his hairs and birds grew from the feathers that flitted from his cape into the breeze.

Humans and followers slipped from the lips of the gods, especially the goddess of the Mundane.

Or, at least, that was what Chrysanthemum had been told.

There was no time to ponder it.

She scanned the page once more, eyes darting over every word and illustration: the explanations of their intelligence, their bloodlust, their cruelty. She knew more about dragons than she had ever wished to know; secrets lingered on every page, something new every time she lay eyes on such a treasure.

Dragons could slumber for weeks. Months.

She had gotten that one right.

An attack would awaken them, especially as prying the mouth open was the only way to reveal their weakness, but light footsteps would not. Human speech could even be ignored. They could snore through shouts and desperation, but magic would rouse them from even the deepest slumber. An inevitability.

Chrysanthemum closed the book.

That was good enough, she supposed. Her magic was subtle, and there were already no animals to communicate with: not a rat, not a dragonfly, not a maggot. And she could be silent. She could creep around the rubble, the dust, and she could *investigate.*

A plan would come to her.

Chrysanthemum packed away her book with as little sound as she could manage, though she knew the dragon could not hear. She tied her bag with a rope, sheathed her sword, and retrieved her bow from the ground, before ensuring she had all her arrows in her quiver.

She listened for the snores again, and found them rumbling just as before. They were thick, hearty, and as deep as the seas of Wavun of Water, as thunderous as a building storm, as bloodthirsty as a beast that fed on copper and flesh. The final was fact.

Chrysanthemum would do everything in her power to rid the city of this beast, tormenting its citizens with a plague of fear. The buildings had already been infected: splattered with ash and knocked by careless, volcanic limbs. Bones scattered the streets, charred beyond recognition.

She did not know whether she would have preferred them to be human or animal. She refused to study each black bone with too keen an eye. She had been caged alongside corpses enough.

Her hesitation slipped away, as if pocketed by a firm hand, and she stepped out from between the two buildings that cradled the alleyway, having hidden her like an infant behind a shield.

The tail lay still.

Chrysanthemum approached. Slow. She followed its curve, its scales like smooth, dried rose petals, if rose petals shone like ice. But the heat that radiated from each pulled sweat from her skin.

Panting, she wiped her forehead with her sleeve, slipping through the gap between the tail and the wall, inches from burning to a crisp. The rumbles made her trip several times, shaking the castle as if it were formed of sticks and twine. But she stayed as upright as she could.

She followed alongside crumbled walls and the fallen paintings of nobles who had once lived in a castle so lavish. Chrysanthemum hoped, in the back of her mind, that the charred bones she found, strewn across the floor, were stone-made and decorative.

Deciding not to ponder that, Chrysanthemum navigated between scattered bricks and shattered glass, and found herself facing a long, clawed foot. Still. Silent. Scaled.

Chrysanthemum took a breath, only wincing a little at the smoky heat of the air, filling her lungs with a thick, itching burn.

The dragon must have been the size of the castle in its entirety.

Did she dare search for its head? Or should she flee, and return once she was far readier? The answers evaded her, sticking to each other like a mouthful of sap, and she loitered on the spot. Her bow, imprisoned in her hand, lowered as her mind raced, scrambling over her options and finding none that suited her. The heat drove her mad.

It was so silent that Chrysanthemum was engulfed by nothing but her own mind, a cacophony she could almost hear. It was so silent, she realised, that the castle had stopped shaking. The only sounds were Chrysanthemum's shuffling footsteps and breaths of desperation and—

The snoring had stopped.

Chrysanthemum's breaths hitched, just as the dragon's foot began to move. She scrambled back, footsteps clumsy, and nocked an arrow before she could think. But what would happen if she fired it?

She could not pierce its scales.

A weakness. A weakness. A *weakness*.

Chrysanthemum needed a weakness, but the only one she knew of was far out of reach and perilous to search for. Did it even know she was there? She had no reason to believe that.

Shit. Shit. *Shit.*

Chrysanthemum lowered her bow, tucking her arrow back into the quiver. She turned, searched the trembling room, and lay eyes on a long, plush seat, positioned just under a painting. She stumbled over to it, boots catching on trinkets and bones, keeping her head raised just enough to watch as the leg and tail slipped through the portion of wall she had yet to pass through.

Where its claws tore through plush carpet and blackened wood, patches of floor burst aflame. Was the dragon in control of that, or was it akin to an out-of-control god, more magic than mind?

The dragon's steps made everything around her shake and slip and shatter. Murky shards of glass coated the floor, dancing with every rumble, though Chrysanthemum's boots were thick enough to merely crunch them underfoot. Paintings dropped, their colours smeared and warped by the rising heat.

Chrysanthemum clamped a hand over her mouth, smothering desperate, panting breaths. Sweat dripped from every exposed patch of skin. Her clothes itched unbearably.

She needed to escape.

As happened often, Chrysanthemum needed to escape. But she had no guards to trick, no nobles to bribe, no pirates-of-Wrath to unlock a cage-door. She had no hope of overpowering such a beast.

Dackon's warning sang in her ears.

The dragon's movements filled the castle with just as much noise as its snores had. It would mask Chrysanthemum's own steps. But she had to be quicker than it was.

She leapt from her hiding spot, dashed across the room, and stumbled. The wall broke her fall, but the sizzling bricks beneath her melting gloves had her screaming, like the intricate patterns were branding themselves across her palms.

The wails from Chrysanthemums lips could not be suppressed.

She fell, backside hitting the smouldering floor, glass cutting through her skirt and slicing her skin like spears. Her quiver slipped from her shoulder, arrows scattering across the floor. Her bow landed far from her hand, and she had no hope of retrieving it, as it burst aflame.

Chrysanthemum panted – every inhale filling her lungs with heat, every exhale spitting smoke into the air that surrounded her – before she cast a wide-eyed look back over her shoulder.

An eye.

In the gap that the tail and foot had once poked through, there was now a giant, open eye. It was solid white, like a pearl of the gods, and stared right into Chrysanthemum's very core.

"*Invasion*," it whispered.

Chrysanthemum scrambled to her feet as if the dragon's word had ignited a fire in her belly. With no thought to how impossible it would be to outrun such a beast, she raced through the gaping holes she had snuck through. Agony filled her to her core.

Burning. Burning. Burning.

Even the smallest of breaths burned: her lungs filled with smoke.

She ran.

She ran, and she escaped the castle. She heard no following footsteps. The pounding in her skull was far too thunderous.

She ran as far as she could. Trees filled her blurred vision, though there was no space left in her for relief. And as soon as she felt the dirt beneath her broken, half-melted boots, every remaining ounce of strength fled from her bones.

And she collapsed.

❋ ❋ ❋

"Are you going to sit still, Miss Clawe?"

Chrysanthemum hissed through clenched teeth, eyes screwed tightly shut. Her hands made fists in her skirt, an attempt at grounding herself, but one that was not particularly effective. She could hardly hear Kaydah over her throbbing head.

"I'm trying, *Miss Latche*." The words took on a teasing tinge, though only as much as she could manage.

When had she last been in such agony?

Kaydah chuckled, dabbing at Chrysanthemum's burns with a potion-laced cloth. It had hurt beyond reason when she had pressed it against the blistering flesh of Chrysanthemum's palms, but that had been the worst of it. Her legs had been next, and – finally – the healing had spread to her neck.

"It's going to hurt most when you drink it," Kaydah said, and dabbed once more, before pulling back her cloth. "Are you ready for that? Or would you like to wait a moment?"

Chrysanthemum huffed, cracking her eyes open, and gave Kaydah a pained, lopsided smile. "It'll hurt like a bitch, either way. I might as well take it now."

"Language."

"You've never spat a curse before?"

Kaydah's lips pressed into a thin line. But, after a moment, the expression twitched, and she lowered her head to chuckle. "I avoid it when I can. But I suppose I don't mind, in certain circumstances."

"Do I have permission to do so now?"

Kaydah gave her flat look, adjusting her glasses. Then, she turned and reached into the bag beside her: clumsily sewn together, with patches of fabrics in every texture and hue. An old project, perhaps? The work of a seamstress not yet grown, kept in Kaydah's clutches out of sweet sentimentality. That was hardly Chrysanthemum's focus, though, especially as the bottles in the bag jingled like bells.

"How do you know which is which?" Chrysanthemum watched as Kaydah retrieved a bottle, cream and speckled with violet dots. "Did you make them yourself? I've never known a human to do so before."

Kaydah froze, before her expression shifted into something closer to shame. "I, uh…"

Chrysanthemum gave a bark of laughter, before flinching, as that only made her chest ache more. "Did you steal them?" she croaked.

"Borrowed."

Chrysanthemum bit her tongue. "Are you going to return them?"

Kaydah placed the bottle on the ground beside her knees. She uncorked it slowly, and lifted it to her nose. As she sniffed, her eyelids fluttered, as if in a single moment of bliss.

"No," she finally said.

"Stolen, then." Chrysanthemum leant back, her eyes flicking over the violet-skin ceiling of the tent, before she looked to Kaydah once more. She half-smiled, though it was more a grimace. "I'll look past it. I have bigger things to worry about."

Kaydah handed her the bottle, and Chrysanthemum lifted it to her lips. She took her first slow sip, like chugging liquid frost, before the potion finally began to soothe. Her eyelids fluttered closed.

Bliss. Almost.

As she drank, Kaydah continued to speak.

"My sister is somewhat of a... thief."

Chrysanthemum's eyes opened, and she lowered the half-drunk potion. She readied to speak, but Kaydah reached out, guiding the bottle back to Chrysanthemum's lips. She chuckled against the glass rim, though obediently continued to drink.

Kaydah wrapped her shawl around her shoulders, her gaze gaining a thoughtful glint. "We needed those skills, once upon a time. She stole from those with too much. But not anymore." She frowned. "It doesn't matter. It is what it is, I suppose. I have no way of returning the potions, not without acquiring knowledge of their owners, and not without risk of imprisonment." She sighed. "I do what I can. I know what some are capable of, but most... it's a guess, at best."

As the final drop landed on Chrysanthemum's tongue, she lowered the bottle and wiped at her mouth with her sleeve, smearing warm ash across her cheek. She sighed, but before she could fix it, Kaydah snatched a scrap from a pile of cloths, leant in, and brushed Chrysanthemum's face, cleaning the grey stain.

Chrysanthemum blinked, a little taken aback, and then chuckled, batting Kaydah's hand away. Kaydah blinked, surprised, as if it had been but an instinct, and then gave a small, sheepish smile.

That round face was burrowing right into Chrysanthemum's heart.

She, too, smiled. "So, there's nothing in that sack that'll aid me in my quest, Miss Latche?"

Kaydah paused, and then shrugged. "I suppose you could experiment, but it is just as likely to find a potion of ice as a potion of strengthening. You could soothe a flame or turn yourself to wood. You could worsen your fate beyond salvation."

Sighing, Chrysanthemum placed her hands on the floor behind her, the flesh tender and stinging, though bearable. "That... unhelpful. But thank you. And thank you, even more so, for the healing. I'm glad you've identified *that* potion, at least."

Kaydah bobbed her head. "Anything for our saviour."

"Not quite a saviour yet, but I'll do everything I can."

Kaydah prodded Chrysanthemum's arm, her soft smile turning playful. "You should be more certain of it! You must have more faith in yourself, Miss Clawe. As much as I do, at least."

"You've met me twice, for barely three hours in total, and you already have such faith in me?" Chrysanthemum chuckled, shaking her head. "You must be careful. Someone may lead you astray."

Those lavender lips curled. "You won't. I know that much."

"I'll do everything in my power not to disappoint you, Miss Latche."

A bout of silence overcame them, accompanied by the sounds of the forest around them: the rustle of twigs and the chatter of ants.

Chrysanthemum's eyes flicked to the closed tent door, billowing in the breeze. Beyond, there was hushed conversation, whispered between citizens afraid to speak too loudly. Their speech was close to incomprehensible, but Chrysanthemum caught a handful of words.

"I've been... working on something," Kaydah said. "I almost wished to wear it myself, but that shall never happen. I know that now. It may be of use to you, Miss Clawe."

Chrysanthemum's focus was elsewhere, her ears perking at something that made her heart jolt, forcing energy through her veins.

She scrambled to her feet, to the startlement of her companion, and did not listen as Kaydah called after her.

Chrysanthemum left the tent, hurrying to the gathering around the campfire: setting the darkening sky aglow, spewing amber light and leaving shadows all around. It gave the impression that the huddled city-folk had tripled in size.

They each rested under the constellation of Beake known by most as the jaws. A beast ready to swallow them whole.

The first of the city-folk to spot her was a child, squeaking and clutching at her mother's patchwork skirt. The rest noticed within moments, and the gasps were similarly alarmed.

As if surrendering, Chrysanthemum raised her hands. "I mean no harm," she reassured. "I just overheard something."

She paused. But no one said another word.

Irritation twinged in her soul.

"Something about the dragon," she clarified. "Something about its—its shapeshifting. I just need to know what was said."

The gathering crowd looked upon her with caution. A few mumbled their hesitance, their derision, and Chrysanthemum found her fingers twitching with a growing impatience. But before anyone could give anything away, or shoo her from their campsite, the child peeked out from behind her mother.

"Mama says the dragon gets small," she whispered.

Chrysanthemum's face softened, and she crouched, though did not step nearer. She offered a smile, hoping her feline eyes were subtle, even in the firelight that made them glow.

"It does," Chrysanthemum said. "What else did your mama say?"

The child glanced up at her wide-eyed mother. After a few agonising moments, the mother swallowed, and then nodded. With a newfound confidence, chest puffed out, the child released her mother's skirt. She took a trembling step in Chrysanthemum's direction.

"It got into Snikett like a little fly. I caught it in my net, but mama told me to let it go." Her face crinkled. "She thought it was a bug."

"I'm glad you let it go," Chrysanthemum said. "It would've been pretty scary if it'd tried to hurt you, huh?"

The child shook her head. "I don't think it could've, miss."

"Oh?"

Another shaken head, though this was far more exuberant. "It couldn't fit through my net. And it couldn't break it." She held up her hand, her fingers only a little apart. "Tiny dragon. Tiny strength."

Was it really so simple? It never was.

Chrysanthemum blinked, her startled mind spiralling, and then rose to her full height, casting a shadow-cape across the dirt.

This time, though, the child was unafraid.

"Tiny dragon, tiny strength," Chrysanthemum muttered. "Huh."

There was a pause, filled not with chatter, nor panicked whispers, but with crackling fire and the rustling of Kaydah following her out of the tent. She held something that clinked like light armour.

Finally, Chrysanthemum grinned. "Good work, little one. I'd say you have the means to be a hero, too."

The child's spine straightened: eyes alight.

"Really?"

"Oh, yes! You've already given me a *very* good idea."

❊ ❊ ❊

Chrysanthemum raced through the streets, heart pounding to the pace of her thunderous footsteps. She turned a corner, dodging a burst of flame that merely brushed against her back.

Had she not been gifted a cloak of scales by Kaydah – hastily finished as Chrysanthemum had relayed her plan to *lure* – the fire would have set her clothes and skin aflame. Instead, the heat made her hiss through clenched teeth, but did not actually harm her.

She continued to race, as quick as she could, with nothing to guide her but those feathered beings that soared overhead.

"Left."

She swerved.

"Duck!"

A set of claws swiped at her head, missing by a metre and tearing into the cobblestones between them. The street trembled like an earthquake, the force launching Chrysanthemum into the air.

She landed – swift and unaffected – and only quickened her pace.

"Listen-listen-listen!" the birds chorused.

They were not talking to Chrysanthemum.

The dragon gave a growl of violent thunder –

nothing even close to speech – accompanied by crackling sparks and the rumbling of a building flame in the back of its throat. Every time Chrysanthemum heard the opening of its giant maw, the urge to turn hit her so suddenly she almost did, despite the risks.

An opening was what she needed. Her new bow was in her hand, an arrow already nocked. But would she be quick enough?

She could not risk it.

As Chrysanthemum turned a corner, she dodged the massive footprint of a beast often the size of a palace. The remains of the street crackled and smouldered, even sparkling with embers in stone. Sweat pooled in her boots every time she stepped too close.

Where was she headed? She could not forget.

She had little time. The scribbled map in the back of her mind was hardly more than murky, like peering into a fog-filled lake, memory far from her area of expertise. But she knew enough.

Left. Right. Left.

Forward until she hit the tavern – beside a butcher, she recalled, with an ever-present stench of burnt flesh and sizzled hair – and then she would have to climb. Down. Down. Down.

It seemed a city often infested with creatures great and small had found its ways to hide. And its ways to trap.

The dragon roared like a giant's empty belly.

Chrysanthemum turned a corner, her shoulder

catching on a wall and sending pangs of pain through her torso and arm. She hissed through clenched teeth, eyes slipping shut for just a moment, and that was when her boot caught on a half-smashed bottle, and she tumbled.

She hit the ground with a thud. Her breaths were slammed out of her, so sudden she almost vomited. Her bow and arrows – her *only* chance of killing such a beast – slipped from her grip, sliding just out of reach.

Chrysanthemum stretched. But her arms burned from overuse.

The thudding of clawed paws against cobblestone streets grew quicker, nearer, though the dragon, at this size, was slow. The rumble of brewing flames grew louder and harsher and crueller.

Houses and stalls crumbled below its feet.

A set of talons landed on Chrysanthemum's shoulder, making her yelp and flail, but it only took moments for her to recognise such claws as harmless: an eagle, soon joined by a dove and a swan and a feathered feline with eyes like her own. They grabbed her by her arms, by her shoulders, and flapped their wings – straining, groaning, hissing desperate pleas and encouragements – and yanked her to her feet.

She wobbled, limbs screaming, and then straightened, her determination returning. But as she began to bend and reach for her scattered bow and arrows, there was another burst of flame.

And it hit her dove.

It had no time to scream. It fell to the streets as ash.

Chrysanthemum did not have the time to mourn. She did not have the time to retrieve her weapon. She simply continued to race.

Her feathered friends cried their despair, but they were courageous, and they followed as she ran. Something about Chrysanthemum's presence made them more than smarter, but stronger, too.

"Right. Left."

The stench of a butcher overwhelmed her. The tavern sat just beside: its door half-open, its chairs thrown through shattered windows, its tables overturned. Victims of the violence of the fleers. And, right between the buildings, there sat a hatch, laying across the ground like a door yanked from its hinges and tossed aside.

This, she knew, would open, if Kaydah could be trusted. It was bolted – heavy and thick – but nothing she could not handle. It was far from the cage that had once kept her.

She did not again need to be rescued by the cruel.

Chrysanthemum panted heavily, and sprinted with as much speed as she could muster. She slid across a smoother patch of street, wet with ash-filled rain, and stopped at the door. She crouched, unbolted, and opened it, allowing her creatures to dive in first, before she followed.

She did not take the ladder and instead leapt into the shadows, rolling as she hit the ground, unharmed by the fall, though the rest of her ached.

She did not bolt the door behind her.

Instead, she sprinted down the long, dark hallway, with no way to see, only echoing whistles and hisses to follow.

"Ahead! Ahead! Ahead!"

She ran.

"Stop! Which way? Left? Right?"

A fork in the tunnel.

Chrysanthemum froze. Not from indecision, nor from fear. Her resolve only strengthened, her breaths heavy and quick. She looked back over her shoulder, peering into the darkness.

The trapdoor was ripped from its hinges, letting in sunlight, and then letting in firelight. In the amber glow, it was impossible *not* to watch as the dragon shrank, from towering, towering, towering like an oak into something only twice her height.

Bubbles frothed from its teeth, glowing like seafoam aflame.

Fearsome. But weaker.

She let out a sigh of relief. Turned. And then sprinted left.

The firelight that followed her was all that illuminated the path ahead, though it soon grew thick and foggy with smoke. Her lungs burned with every breath, though she tried not to inhale unless she absolutely had to.

The beast barely kept her pace, like its body weighed it down. But Chrysanthemum was far from safe. It could catch up, and it had twice the stamina she did. She would never outrun such a creature for long. A creature that had killed more people than days she had lived.

Hours, even.

But she knew where she was going. She just had to reach it first.

"Left!" cawed a blue-tinged hawk, invisible in the dim light.

This place had once been for capture and study. But now the signs were indecipherable, especially at the pace she ran at, and *especially* without the lighting of the lanterns that hung overhead. Dim candles speckled waist-high shelves, though only in every other hallway.

She veered left.

Unlit by the flames that chased her, the path ahead was as dark as night. It could have held any number of threats, and Chrysanthemum would have been none the wiser.

The stench of urine and faeces overwhelmed her senses, making her stumble and gag, but she slammed her hand over her mouth, forcing herself not to vomit. In her revulsion and panic, she could not hear the warnings that sang overhead, and slammed right into a door.

She fell onto her backside, and the hallway was again alight with that bright amber fire-glow.

Chrysanthemum leapt to her feet, though her head ached and bled, and her eyes gave little of use. Her tear-ducts wept from the smoke, her lips dribbling foul-tasting ash.

A door.

Her heart was overcome with relief. It seemed Chrysanthemum had been *right* to trust Kaydah and her potions and her eyes.

When had her instincts ever let her down?

Chrysanthemum needed to get through that door.

She did not bother to check if it was locked. Instead, she raised a leg and kicked the door with one booted foot, every ounce of strength used for this one action. The door flew open.

Immediately, a cacophony hit her with almost as much force as the door had. Squawks. Hisses. Whines.

The clawing of furred beasts against impenetrable metal. Caged. The desperate pleas of blessed creatures unfed for weeks. The keening song of animals surrounded by the warm corpses of their brethren.

For a moment, Chrysanthemum was frozen.

How dare they?

The agony filled her to her core, her eyes stinging, her heart racing, her breaths violent and tremulous.

The pounding of clawed feet brought her back to herself, and she realised what she had to do. She turned, grabbing the door, and a spark of relief emerged when she realised it did, in fact, have an opening: a hole at the very top, with just enough room for birds to fly through.

She gave a calling whistle as she slammed the door shut, and her feather companions soared through without a second thought. They joined the echoing wails at the sight of their brethren.

As soon as she bolted the door shut, something large and metal was pressed into her hands, shaking with magic. A birdcage, empty of all but tacky stains and rust. Bars that blocked magic of every kind. She opened it quickly, pressing the cage against the hole in the door.

And when the dragon shrank to follow through the window, its body filled the birdcage, and Chrysanthemum closed and bolted its door shut.

❊ ❊ ❊

"Do you have a name?"

The dragon gave no answer. It did not look at her – curled up in the cage like something weak and helpless, something far from its true power. It had not tried to spew flames since its capture, as what would be the point? This cage was designed to block the magic within.

"I'm not going to hurt you," Chrysanthemum continued.

The dragon raised its head, its scales like slices of metal. They glowed as it glowered, lighting the room like a flame. It did not believe her in the slightest, though it understood every word.

Chrysanthemum would not have, either, in its place.

"I just want to talk," she said. "I don't want to hurt you. I don't want to hurt anybody, in fact." She chuckled, shifting on the puddle-splattered floor, and leant back on her gloved palms. "Maybe I didn't choose the right path, if that's my mantra. I don't ever want to hurt anybody, isn't that odd? I've been mocked for it, though perhaps that's simply my choice of company."

Her curls bounced as she shook her head, dark bubbles that haloed her sweet-earth face. As warm as the veins below her flesh.

"Pirates," she said. "I've found pirates to be decent company. And I suppose they're drawn to me, too. We entertain one another. And, every once in a while, we're almost allied." She paused. "Do you know of The Fury of the Drowned? Villains, most of all, but their Wrath-captain rescued me, once upon a time. I suppose he has drawn me to pirates altogether, more than the friends I've made on other ships."

The dragon snorted, a curl of smoke slipping from its nostril. It rested its chin on the end of its tail, wrapping around its whole body.

A cage that small was never comfortable.

But the camps of cowering city-folk, dotted on the outskirts of a home unsafe, were not comfortable, either. They were anguished and afraid, mourning those who had not fled quick enough, and Chrysanthemum was staring down at the being responsible for it all.

Kaydah filled her mind: her crinkles of worry,

her gnawed lips, the crescent-moon indents where nails had dug into palms. A Mundane healer, descended from Disease. She was nobler than any other.

Chrysanthemum pursed her lips, before pushing the thought aside, even as conflict curdled in her belly.

She needed to keep her focus on the beast.

"I've never met a dragon before," she said. "I've been scarred by beasts aplenty, vanquished those I could not save, but never a dragon. Some kingdoms don't believe in your kind anymore. I knew, though." She smiled as if she found this amusing, and adjusted her stain-speckled skirt. "I guess I have a sense for these things. Our god has strange magic, doesn't he? He wishes for equality between every creature."

The dragon did not answer that, though a few of the birds tittered their amusement. As Chrysanthemum found herself chuckling, too, her gaze flitted around the room. Every other cage had been emptied.

"Sometimes I wonder why he blessed me," Chrysanthemum mused, merry and mild. "I wasn't born into it, like most followers, but I've been of Beasts for almost as long as I remember. I guess I was lucky." She gave the dragon a crooked smile. "Followers of Beasts are a lot rarer than we used to be. Maybe for the better. We were a violent bunch."

The silence pressed in on her, even as a butterfly

landed on her knee, pressing its tiny face into her skirt. Had she not been able to see it – gold in the fire-like glow – she never would have known of its sweet comfort. Her lips twitched into a softer smile.

"You must've known a lot of followers, huh?" she asked the dragon, though her eyes remained fixed on the butterfly, allowing it to dance across her leg. "How old are you?" She did not expect an answer, though she did not know what she was expecting.

The dragon raised a spiky tail, covering its mouth with the curling tip. Then, it uttered one single, dragged-out word. *"Forever."*

Chrysanthemum jolted. "Forever? That can't be possible." Her eyes were as wide as saucers, though she was unfamiliar with the crockeries of tea. "Have you met our gods?"

The dragon made a quiet sound, smoke curling from the tiniest visible corners of its lips. It took a few moments for Chrysanthemum to identify it as laughter. An odd, crackling bout of laughter.

A second passed.

"Oh!" Chrysanthemum chuckled. "You have a sense of humour?"

It made no other sound.

Chrysanthemum shook her head. "I would've thought a beast like you would be... serious. Cruel. Noble. You hoard treasure; you nestle in mountainous caverns; you live a solitary life. You... do more with your time than torment an insignificant city of humans."

She had certainly never heard of Snikett, and she was well-travelled, not until the woman of the tavern had brought it to her attention. But perhaps that was how dragons had remained so rare, so hidden. They only attacked the insignificant.

That still made no sense. Why would a creature of such power wish to hide? Dragons were prey to no one.

Her expression morphed into something more serious, though she maintained a certain lightness. "What are you doing in Snikett?"

Covering its eyes with the barbed end of its tale, the dragon turned away. It made a soft, huffing sound, and Chrysanthemum could not decide whether it incited pity or frustration.

A strange mix of the two.

It looked helpless in that stained cage. And Chrysanthemum had never been one to turn down a creature in need.

Her eyes closed for a moment, her mind turning like a wheel.

This creature, despite its size and weakness, would remain a challenge to kill. She would need to force its jaws open, act quick enough not to be burned, and jam a blade right down its throat. It would choke on its own blood. A violent death. A torture.

Chrysanthemum shuddered.

She could leave it caged, but a dragon was almost immortal, as immortal as gods, as immortal as time. It would escape. It may take centuries, but its fury would brew and bubble and burst. Once the cage fell apart, or some fool unleashed the beast, it would have stewed in its hatred long enough to be no more than a monster.

Chrysanthemum knew what it was like to be caged for so long, though she had never committed the accused crime.

Should she show it mercy? Would that make a creature such as this show mercy in return, or would it kill her most brutally?

Was that a risk worth taking?

The dragon caught her eye with its own, white pearls staring straight into her soul. It was ancient, teeming with secrets and plight, and yet gave almost nothing away. Chrysanthemum could not look away, either, not until her feathered feline batted her shoulder, hissing like a snake. Neither she nor the dragon flinched.

Chrysanthemum turned, whispered soothingly, and the cat returned to the floor, curling beside her leg with tense limbs and a protective gleam in its eye. She ran her hand down its back, between ash-splattered wings, until it let out a soft, rumbling purr.

She turned back to the dragon, who watched and watched and watched her. Her teeth grazed her tongue, before she gave it a firm stare.

"You aren't getting out of here without my help," she said. "Not for a while, anyway. Why don't we work together? If you agree to leave Snikett, never to return, then perhaps I'll open this cage and release you. It sounds fair, doesn't it?"

The dragon moved its tail just enough that its mouth was uncovered, and it snarled. Steam bubbled from rows of ivory teeth.

Goosebumps freckled her limbs, despite the sweat. She leant in, though did not touch the bars that would melt her flesh from her bones. She smoothed her features. "You aren't getting out of here without my help. You need to work with me, all right?"

The dragon glowered, before its lips parted, though not enough for a glimpse at its throat. Flames brewed behind its teeth.

Was it really so strong to counteract the cage?

The fire remained dim. It was incapable of anything else.

Chrysanthemum shifted backwards, but stared down the dragon with a cool determination. "Kill me," she said, "and there will be no one left to set you free. My body will rot beside yours."

It did not answer, though the glowing in its mouth dimmed into moonlight, before darkening entirely. It glared.

"You can't break the bars, either. You can't grow, and you're not big enough for that kind of strength."

Of that, she was uncertain. But she could not give that away.

The dragon growled with a wolflike fury.

Chrysanthemum raised an eyebrow.

The dragon's teeth glinted as if washed in virgin blood, its eyes shining like ancient pearls, its scales shaped like no other.

Chrysanthemum watched, refusing to back down, before the dragon's eyes slipped closed. It seemed to ponder, for a moment, before it shrank enough that it fit more comfortably in the cage. It could not further change, though it trembled from trying.

The dragon sat up, and stared right into Chrysanthemum's soul, before its tail rose once more, wrapping around its mouth like a bandit's mask. *"You wish to know my why?"*

A nod.

The dragon shifted on the spot, sending streaks of light through the shadows. Every cage was caked in dirt and blood, with an overpowering stench of rot and decay. Dust made the air sparkle.

"I am older than Beake," it finally said. *"I am older by millennia, by more than you can comprehend. And there is no longer anything new to see. Have you ever lived so long, and done all there is to do?"*

"You're... bored?"

The dragon watched her carefully, before it bowed its head. *"You humans like to name things, as foolish as you are. Your words can never define how I am. But that is the term, I believe."*

Dumbfounded, Chrysanthemum stared.

Bored? Could it truly be that simple?

Chrysanthemum's eyes flicked around the room, at each of the creatures accompanying her. A few looked to the dragon with nothing short of hatred. Others were curious, excited, though it was difficult to read the faces of such beasts. A raven was bored, preening its feathers with its beak, whilst a dragonfly watched.

She could not look to them for advice. Animals were simple creatures, though this ancient beast seemed to be the exception.

And yet she had outmatched such a being in a fight.

If she was careless, she would never do so again.

Though she knew of the perils of such feelings, Chrysanthemum found herself almost *sympathetic* for the creature. She knew of its atrocities, and yet her heart was torn in two, swaying back and forth without pause on either side, like an infant in a rocking embrace.

The dragon looked only for entertainment. Perhaps, if she could supply that, she could achieve her goal through *peace*, not through the violence she so despised. Dackon, with his warnings, would have called her naïve, but Chrysanthemum's kindness had never failed her.

And she knew prophecies were far from impossible to break.

Chrysanthemum leant in. "What's your name, ancient one?"

An odd look filled the dragon's eyes, as smoke curled from its cavernous nostrils. *"Names are for humans and gods. Not dragons."*

"I've met animals with names before."

"I am not one of them."

"Do you want one?"

The dragon's gaze fixed onto the gold-winged butterfly as if pondering if it wished, too, for a name. Could it even wish?

Silence lingered alongside smoke. Chrysanthemum had the urge to gag and cough, but she ignored her itching lungs. Though there was little it could do, all she did was watch the dragon.

"No," it said, and that was that. *"But what is yours?"*

Chrysanthemum paused, blinked, and then smiled. "Chrysanthemum Clawe," she said. "It's a pleasure to make your acquaintance."

A rolling, grumbling sound emerged from the dragon's blood-and-ash-stained lips. Laughter, Chrysanthemum realised. Its teeth were parted, though its throat remained exposed.

The knife strapped to her arm ached, but she did not allow it to hold her focus, not when she did not need it. A peaceful solution was in sight.

She shuffled closer.

"Can we come to an agreement, dragon? I won't hurt you as long as you sweat to leave this place, never to return. I'm sure there's better entertainment elsewhere."

"Is there?"

"Oh, certainly! Novels and music and plays! It's a big world out there. It's filled with followers and beasts. Heroes and villains. You'll find something, or someone, to entertain you, without ever having to hurt another soul. I'm sure there's empty castles to slumber in, if that's what keeps you content. Do you ever dream?"

"*I dream. I dream of what used to be. I dream of my gods.*"

Chrysanthemum's excitement dulled into wonder. "It must be odd, having multiple gods to worship. I can't imagine it."

"*Our god of Beasts is my most precious,*" the dragon said, watching the butterfly as if the insect held more power than it did. It certainly held more freedom. "*But I cannot ignore Fire and Change. I was made by Beasts, and yet they bless me, too: more than you can imagine.*"

"If only humans could be more than one."

The dragon went silent, as if the wistfulness in Chrysanthemum's tone had sent strange thoughts through its skull. Then, it shifted closer and bowed, pressing its forehead to the bars.

How strange, to be prayed to by a being so ancient.

It sighed, as soft as toothless gums. "*Let me free, little hero, and I shall hurt Snikett no more. It shall never see me again.*"

Chrysanthemum blinked. "Are you... sure?" Her voice was slow, and as wary as it could get. "How do I know I can trust you?"

"*I am no human, no follower. I am older than the first betrayal. If you do not betray me, our deal shall persist for your lifetime.*"

She pursed her lips, mulling it over.

This... was what she had wished for. A peaceful end to the city's plight: without violence, without slaughter, without death. She and this beast would both survive. Unharmed. They would part ways, and Kaydah and her people could return home. They could rebuild what had been destroyed.

It was a risk. Chrysanthemum knew that.

But her skin had peeled from the burns; her blood had spilled through her lips. She had lost, and she had regained. That was all Dackon's warning foretold. What else was there to fear?

Chrysanthemum's heart was too big not to show mercy to a creature in such a state. A creature with its own heart, mind, beliefs. A creature that wished for so little. Entertainment. She could understand that.

Chrysanthemum locked eyes with the dragon.

"All right," she said. "I'm going to let you out."

"Thank you."

The dragon's voice was so clear, so deep, that it vibrated through Chrysanthemum's body like an earthquake. She shivered, giving herself the illusion that the floor was trembling, too. Her hands hovered between her torso and the cage, before she shifted closer.

"Move back as far as you can," she said, halfway between a suggestion and a command.

The dragon did as it was told, and she shifted even closer, sitting up on both knees. She reached out, slow, testing that the bars were cool enough to touch. They were. With a careful breath, she unbolted the cage, and let the door swing open.

She moved backwards. Her hand itched to grab the knife concealed in her sleeve, though she did not.

The dragon moved with caution, too, taking one step, and then another and another, until it reached the open door. It looked left, right, before its pearly eyes peered right into Chrysanthemum's soul, wide and expressionless. Its smoke-curling breaths – through smouldering nostrils – were the only sounds in that cage-filled room.

It walked through, landing on the stone floor – claws slicing through puddles – and took a deeper breath, this time with lips parting enough to catch a glimpse at its soft, pinkish throat.

The bird closest to Chrysanthemum cawed, panicked, beating its wings as if to seem capable of battling such a beast. Chrysanthemum inhaled, raising her hands as if to calm it, but it was too late.

The dragon rose so it was only on its back two feet, its mouth opening fully. Flames brewed behind its teeth, like a sun on its tongue.

Sweat poured down Chrysanthemum's face.

She had no time to think. She snatched her knife, whipping it right at the beast. It soared through the air, and lodged in the back of the dragon's throat with an agonising, blood-spraying squelch.

The dragon fell backwards, crying out. A terror most primal.

Chrysanthemum reached in and yanked the knife back out. The dragon scrambled back, blood gushing through its teeth and splattering gore across the stone floor. It whimpered and it wailed, but she could just about make out the words nestled between its cries.

"Mercy! I'm sorry, I'm sorry, I'm sorry!"

Chrysanthemum's heart panged.

This would not be a quick death. The dragon was far too powerful for that. An ancient beast could not be felled so easily.

But it *would* be a death.

She lowered her knife, and looked down at the dragon's face, streaked with anguish and agony, and splattered with that still-spraying scarlet. She held her breath, watching it writhe.

Her heart wailed. Tears pricked her marigold eyes, and not just tears from the violent, blood-reeking smoke that poured from its tongue.

With screaming lungs, Chrysanthemum stepped back. "Climb back into the cage," she said, barely above a whisper. "I shall lock it behind you, leave, and then return with a potion of healing. Do this, and you'll survive. I shall show you mercy."

The dragon whimpered.

For a moment, it looked too weak to agree *or* rebel, but then, meekly, it crawled back over to the cage and climbed inside. Trembling.

And Chrysanthemum locked the door behind it.

✢ ✢ ✢

Chrysanthemum traversed the empty city with almost more caution than she had held when the dragon had been an active threat. She had no creatures circling overhead – they were watching their prisoner, after all – and she was slow, steady, pensive.

As she passed a house with an overgrown flowerbed – vibrant leaves uneaten by the insects chased away – she pondered how to heal the dragon without risking herself in the process. As her eyes darted over a park decorated with animal bones – a deterrent, perhaps – she wondered if healing such a creature was even the right move. And as she dodged a scuttling, gold-legged spider, she almost did something she had never before done. She almost prayed to her god.

But she did not.

She had a feeling she knew exactly what he would say, though she had never once spoken with him, had never once wished to. He would not advocate for unnecessary slaughter. The lack of followers of Beasts, after their millennia of violence, was enough of an indication.

Chrysanthemum had let the dragon go, but things had changed, though barely hours had passed since that moment. Did she dare to free it again, when it could attack once more? But could she kill it?

She could not, she decided, as she descended into the tunnels, holding a lantern in one hand and a bottle in the other: cream, violet, and almost full, as she had only taken a swig.

As she grew closer to the room of cages, the heat grew heavy. Her clothes stuck to her skin, though her shirt and skirt were loose enough, the latter with dampened edges from puddles across the stone floor. She wiped the back of her hand against her forehead, and finally opened the door, entering to the relief of those who stood guard.

The dragon raised its head, eyes anguished and dim. Blood dripped from its glistening teeth.

Chrysanthemum looked it over, brow furrowed, but it did not seem on the brink of death. Not yet. It would die if abandoned, most certainly, if it were left without healing, but that may take *days*.

She breathed a sigh of relief, and then plopped onto the floor, crossing her legs underneath herself.

"Are you all right?"

The dragon answered with only a glower.

Chrysanthemum shifted on the spot and raised the swirling, shimmering bottle. "The dust of a jewel, the breath of a child, mixed with magic and more. You'd need a powerful blessed coin to get your hands on such a thing, ordinarily. Do you know what this can do?"

The dragon straightened, its eyes locking onto the bottle.

Desperation filled those pearls.

"This will heal you. It healed me, too." Chrysanthemum lowered the potion. "But I haven't decided if I'm going to share it just yet."

The dragon snarled, but it came out half a groan.

"If I heal you, and leave you in this cage, you'll eventually escape. You'll find me, and you'll kill me." Chrysanthemum placed the bottle in front of her, placed her hands behind her, and leant back. "If I heal you, and I let you out, you might still kill me. You'll have no reason not to. I won't be able to fight you off *or* trick you again." The swirling stench of blood and smoke made her nauseous. "Of course, I could leave you to die, or even speed up the process. It would take very little."

Sparks flew from the nostrils of the glaring dragon.

"You see my dilemma, don't you?"

The room was as silent as a coffin. Both follower and dragon did not even seem to breathe, their eyes locked in a furious stare.

Chrysanthemum leant in. "What would you do, in my position?"

The dragon did not give an immediate answer, but Chrysanthemum knew it would, no matter who much that may worsen its pain. And, as if their god had bound their minds, she knew *exactly* what it would say.

"I would kill me," it grumbled, before coughing up smoke.

Crimson sprayed from its mouth, splattering across her cheek.

Without breaking eye contact, she wiped away the hot blood with her sleeve. "Yes," she said. "I suspect you would."

Chrysanthemum's mind churned with the same violence as her stomach. The thought of killing a creature as sentient as it was made her eyes sting. The thought of leaving it caged, when it would, one day escape with a vengeance, was hardly more appealing. And the thought of letting it go made her fear what damage it would do next, especially when it had already attacked again.

It was a noble, intelligent creature, acting out of boredom, not cruelty. Did it deserve to die?

She had no other choices. And no one else to turn to.

Her eyes closed. *Shit.*

Chrysanthemum reopened her eyes, her vision taking a moment to adjust, even in the dim dragon-light. "I can't do that," she said. "Gods, I... I think I know what I need to do."

The dragon shifted back as she shifted forward, meeker than a dragon should have been. But when she plucked the potion from the ground, its ears perked. She uncorked it, before tossing the cork aside, and held the bottle between her torso and the bolted door of the birdcage. The potion's lavender scent overtook the stench of sizzling blood.

"Do promises mean anything to dragons?"

"I seldom meet another." It coughed. *"I have not in centuries. Who am I to make promises to?"*

"That's not an answer. Does a promise mean anything to you?"

There was a beat.

The dragon gurgled a sigh. *"It never has,"* it said. *"But it could, I suppose, in the right circumstances."*

Chrysanthemum did not know if she could believe it. But she did not have the time to deliberate so fiercely. She could not wait, not when she could see the blood dripping from its lips, feel the desperation leaking from the its body, and, in some way, feel its pain as if it were her own.

"Promise me you'll leave these people," she said. "That you will take your fire and your fury, never to darken their doorstep again."

"I promise."

Did it know what a promise meant? If only she had magic of Truth, intermingling with the blessing of Beasts that spiralled through her bones. If only she could hold more magic than one.

Humans could never achieve such a thing. It would most likely destroy them, though of that she was uncertain. A blessing like that was reserved for whichever ancient, dragon-like beings remained.

Chrysanthemum reached out with her empty hand, pausing to test the heat of the metal, before she unbolted the cage. The rusted door creaked open. Her feathered friends watched, her golden butterfly utterly still, and she could sense more than half wishing to flee, and the rest so enraptured that the thought had never even crossed their minds.

She could not focus on them.

The dragon crawled closer and opened its

mouth.

Chrysanthemum was struck by the strange realisation that she had *power* over this ancient creature – born at the dawn of creation – that it was utterly at her mercy. Its mangled throat was presented to her, with the knowledge that she could worsen it all with the twist of a blade.

She paused, hesitant, before she poured the entirety of the potion down the dragon's gullet, making a strange, sizzling sound, like rain against a hot cauldron.

Then, she placed the empty bottle back down beside her, and watched as the dragon closed its mouth, already strengthening. She watched, hand on blade, as it twitched and writhed and breathed like its agony was worsening, before fading away.

She watched. And she did not lock the cage door, though half of her wished to desperately.

Once it appeared to be at full strength, they locked gazes.

She waited.

"I will find entertainment elsewhere," it said, *"as I promised."*

Its words were murky and vague, but heavier than stone. They whispered reluctance and gratitude, and condescension aplenty, like a god talking to its most foolish follower. Chrysanthemum's heart dropped; her breaths were yanked from her lungs.

"You're going to attack another city," she whispered.

"I did not promise I would not."

"No." Her voice grew. "That—that was implied!"

"No, it was not."

Chrysanthemum opened and closed her mouth a few times, words refusing to emerge through the cage-bars of her teeth, as if they, too, feared the dragon. Gods. What had she done?

The dragon stared right into the depths of her soul. And, for once, she found she could not read the creature's face. But it did not seem malicious, nor mocking, nor even mirthful. It simply watched.

"I must find entertainment somewhere. I have little else to do."

"You could come with me."

The words startled Chrysanthemum just as much as they startled the dragon. It straightened, tail freezing mid-swish, and her spine straightened, too, as if lightning filled her to her core.

What she was doing?

A fondness for such a creature was a foolish thing to have, and trust was even more so. But how could she not?

She continued before she had the time to truly ponder. She could have stopped herself, she supposed, but it seemed she wished to know what she was thinking just as much as the dragon did.

"There's nothing more entertaining than an adventure. And I'm always having an adventure. There are princesses to save, pirates to battle, magic in every kingdom. That's what it means to be a hero. You meet people; you help in any way you can; you learn new things. And you do something *meaningful* with your life. I mean, what's nobler than heroism? You can't find anything more just."

Chrysanthemum paused, her mind catching up with her words. But she did not have the will, nor the desire, to rescind her offer. She thought, and she thought, and then she straightened once again, meeting those ancient eyes.

"Come with me," she said, as smooth as skin. "And you'll have all the entertainment you need, and none of the cruelty."

To her startlement, the dragon seemed to ponder it, tilting its head one way and then the other. Finally, it crossed the small space between them, brushing its nose against Chrysanthemum's skirt as if it could sense her veracity in the wrinkles of her clothes.

She did not move except to squeeze the knife in her sleeve. "Try it," she said. "You can always leave. That's what must be so wondrous about being a dragon. You'll always be able to fly away."

There was a pause, before the dragon sat back on its hind legs.

"Show me that this is worth my time," it said. *"And do not betray me, little hero of Beasts. I am no fool."*

Though her nerves were alight – whispering its warnings through her mind – some small relief spiralled through Chrysanthemum, and she could not help but smile. "All right," she said. "I'll show you."

* * *

"Are you certain it's safe to walk here?" asked the damsel.

"Of course," answered the saviour.

Chrysanthemum chuckled as they wandered the scarred streets, dotted with fractured pits, crumbled bricks, and charred-and-chewed debris. Her left hand held her knife, tossing and catching it like nothing was simpler, whilst her other was buried in her pocket, with the tiniest of dragons wrapped around her little finger.

Kaydah, and the rest who filled the streets of Snikett, navigated their homes with caution, inspecting the ruins of whatever buildings remained. They gathered in mournful circles, salvaging what they could, though some tried for merriment.

They would struggle, for a while, but they would be fine.

"Do you know, in all the years I've lived, that I've never once left Beake?" Kaydah accepted Chrysanthemum's arm, allowing her to guide her around a puddle. "I've hardly left Snikett, too."

Chrysanthemum chuckled. "Well, did *you* know, in all the years I've lived, that I've never once had a home?"

As Kaydah released her arm, she cast

Chrysanthemum an odd look, pulling her in with those violet eyes. "Never?"

"Not at all. Not unless you'd consider a prison to be a home."

That had Kaydah halting. "Oh?"

Chrysanthemum danced back, tossing her knife into the sky again, as if a gift for the Air. Sunbeams painted the blade with iridescence, before it landed back into her palm.

She looked to Kaydah with a grin. "Don't fret. I didn't deserve it."

"I wasn't *fretting*."

"What would you call this, then?" Chrysanthemum mimicked Kaydah's look of concern, though exaggerated it greatly. Then, she broke. "Do not further fret. I forgive you."

Kaydah rolled her eyes. "Well, if you *forgive* me, dear lady…"

"I would forgive you for anything."

"As I do with you. Your prior imprisonment does not bother me in the slightest." Kaydah's brow then furrowed. "My sister has had enough brushes with it, but she always returns home in the end."

"I hope to meet her someday. I know some pirates she may find kinship with. Perhaps I'll make an introduction."

"I'd rather steer her from such people, if you don't mind. Pirates make for dangerous company. Even with my wishes for freedom, for… adventure, I would never turn to such a kind."

Chrysanthemum bit her tongue to avoid

argument, instead running the pad of her thumb over the scaled spine of the dragon: warm, smooth, but almost sharper than her knife. As their walk resumed, they dodged children playing with the broken toys in the streets, observed by parents with dark circles under their eyes.

With a chuckle, Kaydah watched them pass, before turning back to Chrysanthemum, wearing a smile of sweet caution. "And you're sure Snikett is entirely... uninfested?"

"It's perfectly safe," Chrysanthemum said. She smiled: a tease. "Do you have no faith in me, Miss Latche?"

Kaydah laughed, fuller and sugar-sweet, her petal-locks bouncing like flowers in an earthquake. "I think, at this point, Miss Clawe, you may call me Kaydah. The formalities no longer matter."

"All right, Kaydah. Then you can call me Chrysanthemum."

"Oh, it's a bit of a mouthful. Chrys, perhaps?"

Chrysanthemum's elbow bumped Kaydah's with as little strength as possible. "You aren't the first to try calling me that."

"Oh? Have you turned down the others?"

"Every single one."

Kaydah adjusted her owlish glasses. As sunlight streaked through them, it became clear they were not formed from sheets of glass, but of several tiny scales, clearer than diamonds. "We've been through much together, Miss Clawe. My potions and my cloak are how you won. Have I not earned such a privilege, or am I but one of many damsels?"

With a low hum, Chrysanthemum feigned deep thought.

Finally, Kaydah giggled, leaning back. "I jest, I jest. I shall call you whatever you wish me to, Chrysanthemum, no matter the complexity."

Chrysanthemum laughed, circling around Kaydah with the light feet of a field mouse. Her companion twirled to keep track of her, skirts billowing in the ash-scented breeze, before growing unbalanced and stumbling. Chrysanthemum caught her easily.

"I'll make an exception," she said.

"An exception? Oh, have I really earned it?"

"Without doubt."

Again, their walk resumed, merrier than ever, and they turned another corner, crumbling turrets rising into sight. The walls had massive holes, leaking stained rugs and broken furniture. Their barred windows were gaping jaws with jagged teeth. Most of the damage was irreparable; the rest would take years, at least, though the castle had been made to outlast the city surrounding it.

Chrysanthemum's stomach churned with guilt. But she had done the right thing. She knew that. Never would vengeance be right; never would vengeance be her chosen path.

Her fingers curled around the dragon's tail.

"As you said, you helped defeat the beast. You welcomed me, you mended me, and you gave me your last healing potion, just to help in my... final battle."

Kaydah hummed, thoughtful, as she gave a slow nod. Something unsettled crossed her face. "And you are certain the dragon's gone?"

It curled around Chrysanthemum's finger, listening intently, though it made not a sound. Its scaled belly was smooth and almost too hot to be bearable. But Chrysanthemum wished not to lose track of it, though that was not what she had told the now-tiny creature.

"Certainly. I wounded it, and though it fled, it would never survive such a blow." She swallowed the unsteady lump in her throat: formed by the falsehoods she would usually so despise. "I know Beasts, Kaydah. It won't hurt your city, or any city, again."

Kaydah wore a look of uncertainty, before her shoulders relaxed, and she gave another smile. "That is a relief." She stopped in the middle of the street, between a bickering pair and a tavern with only half its bricks. Chrysanthemum stopped, too. "Am I keeping you, Chrys? If there's anywhere else you wish to go, feel free to do so. I don't want to keep you from anything important."

The breeze made her petal-locks flow like water, the sunbeams making her speckled freckles glitter. She was, for a moment, more captivating than the broken city around her.

Chrysanthemum was always one for a damsel in distress, especially when they turned out to be nothing of the sort.

She laughed, before she nudged Kaydah's arm. "I think you're plenty important." She sheathed her knife and hooked her elbow through the crook of Kaydah's arm. "I promised I'd walk you home, and I shall do just that. Promises are important to keep."

A gust of smoke curled around her finger. A chuckling huff.

Chrysanthemum did not allow herself to react to it.

Kaydah laughed, and the conversation resumed as they journeyed between streets in various stages of disrepair, the castle remaining ever in sight as they curved around it. They passed monstrous footprints, taverns offering beast-stew and fried wings, and gaggles of ragged children. As they journeyed past mirthful mourning, they discussed everything Chrysanthemum could think of but the dragon in her pocket.

Her feathered friends had returned to the forest, unwelcome by the city-folk terrorised by such a terrible beast. Chrysanthemum had wished not to worsen it, though distaste filled her to her core.

And, as they grew closer to where Kaydah's home lay, they also grew closer to the front of the castle, to the grand, towering gates, and the ruins that smouldered beyond repair. It had become the dragon's home, after all. It had been ruined more than everything else.

Chrysanthemum could not imagine the dungeons beneath, nor did she wish to. The belly of the dragon grew a little too hot.

Gathered around the broken gate, the nobles were almost more eye-catching than the home that had been destroyed. They were dressed in amethysts, rubies, and sapphires, each embedded in extravagant furs and jewellery of bone. They carried treasures and meaningless trinkets, and stood beside a carriage with silent, well-groomed horses.

As the pair grow closer, Kaydah leant down and mumbled into Chrysanthemum's ear. "They weren't in the camps," she said. "They found some nearby town, forced them to take care of them, though I suppose they *did* offer rewards in return."

"That doesn't surprise me."

"They—oh! Oh, don't look."

The final words were hissed, Kaydah tugging Chrysanthemum further down the street as a light-haired lord looked their way, his face splattered with salt and disdain. Chrysanthemum did not shift nor soften her gaze, but did allow Kaydah to pull her further away.

"They're not so bad." Chrysanthemum chuckled, giving Kaydah a teasing look. "Well, they're cruel, I suppose. But they're harmless."

Before Kaydah could respond, a booming voice echoed over the ordinary bustle in the streets. "You're to fix our castle first!" came the demand of the light-haired lord. "What is a city without its nobles, its guardians? We are to come first, understand?"

Chrysanthemum's nose wrinkled.

The dragon's breaths were warm against her fingertips, growing hotter with every passing moment. A warning, perhaps. But she had yet to have the need to pull away. Instead, she ran her fingers over the scales as a careful, soothing response.

All is fine.

Those closest to the lord – his family, his servants, the remainder of his guards – attempted to placate him, each in various states of fear, irritation, and sympathy. They pouted and they simpered, offering the treasures in their arms, and it almost began to work, until one burly man with the looks of a blacksmith crossed the street.

The lord's face contorted with fury. He raised a hand, pointed, and a pair of his guards lunged, dragging the man towards him.

He began to bellow in the blacksmith's face, spittle flying from his lips like sea-spray from a sea-beast. His demands were cruel, his threats even more so, and Chrysanthemum's heart panged with rage.

Who was he to spit such curses?

She took an instinctive step in the man's direction, but Kaydah tugged her back with a startling strength. "This isn't your battle," she whispered. "There's no point in fighting, not when you'll lose. This is no dragon, no vanquishable foe."

Chrysanthemum tensed, almost immovable.

Then, she exhaled, dragging her hand down her face.

She knew when a battle was futile, when there was nothing left to win. A noble was no reasonable beast.

But something caught her attention before she could talk, almost enough to tear her from her rage entirely. A sharp pain on her thumb – a burn so sudden it made her hiss and snatch her hand from her pocket, leaving the dragon to warm the fabric that pressed against her leg.

"Forest. Now."

She jumped, startled, and Kaydah looked to her with wide eyes.

"Are you all right, Chrys?"

Chrysanthemum took a moment to orient herself – shit, shit, *shit* – before she nodded. She needed not to anger the dragon, not until she was certain it had become something good, something to *trust*.

A familiar dance from one set of morals to the other.

She had done it all before.

And she could not risk failure, not when the dragon could slay thousands in the span of a minute. Not when she had just encouraged the people to make their returns.

"Of course!" She tried not to grit her teeth, hiding the sizzling flesh of her hand. "But I think I must take my leave. I have things to attend to, things that… slipped my mind. I'm truly sorry, Kaydah. It was wonderful to meet you, more wonderful than every adventure at once."

Chrysanthemum lay it on a little thick, but she loved to indulge in a little charm, every once in a while.

Kaydah gave her a curious look, brimming with sweet suspicion, and then a soft, sad smile. "It was wonderful to meet you, too, Chrys. I hope you return to me someday."

"I hope so, too."

Even in her current state, distracted by the steady charring of her skirt, Chrysanthemum gave Kaydah a charming smile. Then, she reached out with her unharmed hand, and took Kaydah's into her own. She bowed and pressed the lightest of kisses to her knuckle.

Akin to a butterfly on a treasured tuft of grass.

Kaydah made a sound halfway between a gasp and a giggle, and when Chrysanthemum looked back up to meet her eyes, she was pleased to see such warm, flustered cheeks.

But she could not focus on them for more than a moment. Her pocket was too infested with heat, a bundle of plight in her skirt.

She straightened, and then smiled.

"I must go, Kaydah. If you'll excuse me."

"Of course. But I do have something for you first."

Chrysanthemum raised an eyebrow – though her heart raced with awareness of her dragon's impatience – before Kaydah took her bag of potions from where it hung from her shoulder. She held it out.

The bottles jangled like bells, though whether they were the tolls of a marriage or a funeral was uncertain.

Chrysanthemum blinked. "You're... giving those to me?"

"I have no use for them, not when I don't know which is which, and especially as I will likely never leave Snikett again. You'll find proper use for them, I'm sure."

A precious gift. A healing disease in every prison of glass.

Chrysanthemum stared, and then smiled, taking the bag. "You really are a treasure, Kaydah." She slung the strap over her shoulder. "I cannot wait to return to Snikett someday. Try not to get into too much trouble in the meantime, all right?"

"Oh, I doubt I shall. I am not quite the adventurous type, as you know. And the dragon shall never return, after all. Life will soon slip back into normality, I'm sure."

* * *

Chrysanthemum's pace quickened with every street she passed.

Many city-folk called after her, though most only had a vague idea of her identity. But she could not stop, not while her skirt began to smoulder and char, getting closer to flesh with every moment passed.

Shit. Shit. *Shit.*

She had to lead it far. She had to soothe it quickly.

Her heart pounded, her teeth clenched, and, though pain descended upon her like a vulture to a corpse, she did not stop until she had passed the treeline and journeyed deep enough into the forest that she could not be overheard by any mortal.

Slumped against a tree, she cried out the moment she could, and reached into her pocket. She grabbed the dragon by its papery wing – a scorching, unbearable heat – and yanked it out, tossing it aside.

It hissed in fury, growing to the size of a wolf before it could even hit the ground. Its claws tore the dirt and grass as it slid, rife with a rage that could only ever belong on such a face. It growled like it did not have the ability to communicate.

"What is it?" Chrysanthemum demanded, her hand on her knife, though she knew it would do little good. "What did I do?"

The dragon growled for a moment longer, before it took a step towards her, crouched low, though its wings were poised and ready to take flight. *"You think these mortals are worthier of the castle than I?"*

Chrysanthemum stared, open-mouthed, almost more bewildered than she was on edge. "What? Why does that matter?"

With a snarl, the dragon stalked forward.

She stepped back.

"Not all mortals are the same," she said. "Sure, there are cruel humans, cruel followers, but that is no reason to attack them all. And do you even care about that? I thought—"

"*You claim to battle villains, yet cower before nobles? You break your promises. You are not who you claim to be, faux-hero.*"

Chrysanthemum's blood boiled, pushing up against her flesh.

"I'm no faux-hero—" she began.

"*What do you call it?*" the dragon spat. "*A hero enacts justice.*"

"I enact justice! Do you know the people I have saved? Hundreds, thousands, more. I stopped you —"

"*You placated me. And you disappointed me before our partnership had even begun.*" It took another stalking step forward. "*Do you see our god anywhere, Chrysanthemum?*"

She stared: mouth open, breaths stolen.

"*He has abandoned you. And so must I.*"

Chrysanthemum held out her hands – a placating gesture, despite her bubbling frustration. Who was the dragon to speak to her in such a manner? She was a hero; she always had been!

Heat radiated from the glimmering beast. Sweat dripped from her every patch of skin, her breaths shallow and filled with smoke.

"*Your kind of unworthy of anything more than entertaining me.*"

"That's not—"

"*You think you will delight me with your quests, but*

allow such pests to do as they wish? I have met heroes. They fight whoever they must."

A dagger of guilt pierced Chrysanthemum's heart, dragged down to mix with the furious shame in her gut. Should she have done more? Should she have begun a battle she had no hope of winning? That was never the right move. She knew that now more than ever.

A part of her wished to stand her ground. She knew the dangers of giving in to such a beast.

But, even more so, she had to *placate* it. She had no choice.

Chrysanthemum took a slow, deep breath, though the smoke itched her lungs. She remained calm, even as the dragon glowered and snarled.

"This is good," she soothed. "You have a *heart*. Don't you understand? You hate these nobles, and I hate them, too. We'll *take down* villains such as them. That's what I do!"

Its eyes narrowed. *"You're going to take down these monsters?"*

Chrysanthemum opened and closed her mouth.

Was it really the best move, to further destroy a city already in such disrepair? Would that bring any good to its people? And they were only nobles, not beasts to overcome...

"Well—"

The dragon leapt towards her. Her knife slipped from her sleeve, landed in her palm, and then slashed. It did nothing against such impenetrable scales, made for violence, made to live forever.

Instead, the dragon caught the blade between its teeth, wrenched it from her grip, and spat it aside. It slid across the mud, hitting a log. Far out of reach.

"You are not who you claim to be, Chrysanthemum. If you are no hero, perhaps you are no entertainment, either. I might as well finish what I started. How many damsels can I burn?"

Chrysanthemum leapt through a gap between the dragon and a bug-flecked bush, ducking under the branch of a thorn-nest tree. She grabbed the handle of her sword, unsheathing it in one swift movement, and spun to face the dragon again.

It doubled in size, biting right through the blade. She dropped it immediately, kicking aside the remains, and reached for another hidden knife. She was disarmed just as violently.

Sparks scattered across her bare hands. As they landed, sinking in and sizzling, she hissed through gritted teeth, eyes watering.

As the dragon prowled closer – its claws pulling roots from dirt-homes – Chrysanthemum stumbled back, her burning hands outstretched. "Please! Just listen to me! They don't deser—"

"I don't care what they deserve. And you don't, either."

"Even if you kill me, you'll be stopped eventually. There are so few of your kind for a *reason*. There's never a shortage of heroes. And if you want entertainment, there's nothing like an adventure. Please—"

"I have not lived since the age of the gods by listening to heroes and their whines. I gave you a chance, the first I have given in centuries, and that is the only mistake I have ever made."

The dragon leapt at her, dragging its claws down her chest, tearing her shirt and skin and knocking her to the forest floor. She wailed. Was this how she would die? After everything, did she deserve—

Before the dragon could bite her or burn her or tear her limb-from-limb, her hand found its way into the bag of potions. Her fingers closed around the neck of the nearest bottle, and she smashed it against the beast's scaled head.

The potion splattered across both the dragon and her arm.

The follower and beast screamed in unison. Their agony filled the sky as Chrysanthemum lost the ability to move that arm, to even twitch her fingers. With her other hand, she tore her sleeve from her skin, and watched as the flesh of her sword-arm hardened.

It spread from finger to elbow, before the pain was snatched away, as if by the hand of a god. Her right arm, sizzling, was now far from flesh and blood and bone. Instead, it was solid, immovable.

Wooden.

And when she looked back up, she found herself eye-to-eye with something equally still, like an hourglass refusing to spit sand. It was as if there had never been an ounce of movement in the dragon's body.

It was still. It was wooden.
It was dead.

* * *

The jagged wooden claw, streaked with silver like ancient hair, fit perfectly in the palm of her hand. Had one not known of its origin, they would have thought it to be none other than a twig – far from a keepsake, far from memorable. But Chrysanthemum knew.

Someone would have done it eventually.

She knew that. She just wished she had not been the one to.

She had not even tried to, not really.

But would she have survived had she splashed the dragon with anything but *that*? Should she have survived?

None of the potions had fixed her arm. And nothing she did returned the feeling to the limb that was now, for all intents and purposes, dead. It could not even move. And the thought of returning to Kaydah made her even closer to spewing vomit down her clothes.

Chrysanthemum tried not to think about it, and instead kept her arm hidden by her sleeve, and her hand hidden by a thick green glove, almost like encasing it in leaves, though she tried not to think about that. She pocketed her hand, and looked across the port with wary eyes.

She was sure she would find passage on one of

those ships. And, frankly, she did not care where she ended up, just so long as it was in one of the seven islands in this part of Ungode. There were quests everywhere, villains to vanquish that she would not be so torn about battling.

Her eyes focused on a large vessel with golden sails – shimmering like sunbeams – and a crew that were clearly crooks, rapscallions, pirates. Their clothes were ragged, though their bodies were decorated with jewels and jewellery in similar shades as the sails.

Pirates would lead her to trouble.

And that was exactly what Chrysanthemum needed.

She wandered in its direction, crossing the dock it was tied to, and caught a glimpse of this ship's title, carved into its side with a dagger.

The Everdrowned.

A familiar name.

Pirates, as suspected. They were not quite so notable as The Crimson Dead, nor many of the other ships that had once held her. But Chrysanthemum knew of it.

There was no one on that ship who was not of the Mundane.

Would Chrysanthemum, a follower, be allowed to set foot on such a vessel? She supposed there was no harm in trying. Even with her wooden arm, weighing her down and filling her blood with splinters, she had some advantage over humans as a whole.

She loitered, pondering, though soon made up her mind.

Whistling, Chrysanthemum boarded the ship, and found many gazes locking onto her in an instant. There were chuckles, taunts, and warnings, but the crew had yet to make a move to attack her, had yet to even strike up a conversation.

She maintained a distance, and scanned those who watched her.

Her eyes locked onto a familiar set of black braids, accompanying a cool brown face, tucked behind an ear with one silver earring: almost gold in the amber glow of sunset.

For a moment, Chrysanthemum was startled. Then, she was relieved.

And, finally, the pair locked gazes.

A new adventure was being handed right to her.

A FANG AT THE THROAT

LUCAH SHOT

The kiss smeared blood across Lucah's cheek, and that was what tore him from slumber.

His eyelids fluttered, his mind alight, though they did not yet open, lashes twitching like spider-legs. His long black hair, free of its braid, was fanned across the pillow: spilled ink, much alike the scarlet stains that decorated the bed in its entirety.

A cool hand brushed Lucah's jaw, like he was something precious, delicate. Fragile. It traced shapes across his pale skin, scraping nails over lips, before, finally, the fingers slid down and grasped Lucah's throat. His eyes opened, and he met the gaze of the man who lay beside him, half-covered by the blanket draped over them.

The room swayed slowly as the ship rocked, but Lucah paid attention to nothing but his captain, Dackon, who had pushed himself up onto his elbows. Red hair spilled off his shoulders like a waterfall, dotted with the occasional tiny braid, and his eyes were the same solid rubies they always had been.

Lucah had been in The Crimson Dead's crew for nine years now, and Dackon had never aged a day.

He had Lucah to thank for that.

Their mutual magics of Blood bestowed great powers upon them: powers they could only gain from and give to each other.

If only followers of their kind were not so rare.

Lucah stared up at him, blinking slowly as the sleep still misted his eyes. He gave a lazy smile, displaying pointed ivory teeth, and could do nothing but whisper the first words that came to mind. "Bite me."

Dackon did not answer. He, instead, raised an eyebrow.

"Bite me, *please*," Lucah corrected himself.

Dackon ran a finger over one of the scars on Lucah's throat: slow, deliberate, like he was pondering which portion of flesh to sink his teeth into. His lips parted, and as Dackon ran his tongue over four rows of bloodied fangs, Lucah did the very same thing.

Lucah could not track the movement of Dackon's solid eyes, but he could feel the weight of his gaze, like there was nothing more captivating than his first mate's teeth.

"The blood of Blood holds a power unknown even to me," Dackon said, his voice rumbling and deep. His words gripped Lucah by the soul, as if nothing else had ever been quite so important. "Yours fuels my soul, my body, in a way no ordinary blood ever could – in a way no other soul could steal from you. Yours keeps me alive more than any potion ever could. And mine warps your mind."

Lucah nodded. "Yes, captain." He dared not move, lest he shatter whatever was building between them. "I will give everything I am to keep you. You may drink me until I am dead."

Contemplative, Dackon paused, before his finger settled on a particular spot on Lucah's throat. "That won't be necessary."

Dackon's fingers curled around Lucah's neck, and then tugged him closer, capturing his lips in a bruising kiss. Lucah melted, overwhelmed with bliss, and almost could not move, though managed to grasp each of Dackon's arms, the bare muscles thick beneath his fingertips.

And as Dackon deepened the kiss, tongue slipping between teeth, Lucah thought of nothing more than him, him, *him*. Dackon was his captain, his lover, his master, his most beloved. He would do anything for him. He would kill, he would torture, he would *die* for his captain.

He would die by Dackon's blade and Dackon's blade alone. The thought of anything more, anything less, filled him with agony.

Dackon's lips were stolen away.

Lucah gasped for breath. A whine built in his throat, before the mouth returned, simply pressed to his jawline instead. The lips travelled down Lucah's neck, inciting an entirely different kind of whine, until, finally, there was the graze of teeth.

A pause.

The air was thick. Lucah could hear nothing but

his heartbeat.

"Please," he whispered, and Dackon sunk his teeth into his neck.

The bite was as blissfully agonising as it always was, and the blood flowing from him to Dackon made his head spin and heart flutter. His vision blurred, especially in the darkness of the room: the captain's cabin, where Lucah lay every night, whether he was accompanied by his captain or not. All that illuminated the dark, blood-splattered walls was the sunrise streaming through the open window.

It carried a blood-scented breeze, tinged with sea-salt, fresh fishes, and rot. A sweet stench. Almost.

Iridescent spots flashed in the corners of his vision.

Dackon pulled back, and Lucah jolted, gasping for breath as if the bite had suffocated him, though he was sure he had been panting the whole time. His hand flew to his wound, heart pounding, blood gushing through his fingers, filling him with something akin to fear.

Dackon raised a bone-white hand to his teeth, and bit down with just as much violence. Then, he allowed Lucah to drink from his wound.

Bliss filled him to his core, like there was nothing else inside him, like he was floating amongst the stars, the heavens, the gods. Like he was stuffed with cotton and gold. Like he was empty of soul.

He was vaguely aware of Dackon pulling back, before touching him once more. Dackon placed a hand on Lucah's weeping wound, and the skin knitted itself back together. The flesh would scar.

Lucah did not care.

Lucah did not care about anything, not until Dackon pulled away, pulling another whine from Lucah's lips, but one that bordered more on pathetic. Dackon did not respond, especially as Lucah could make no more sound: dazed and blissful, most of all, but with a fuzz to his vision and a pain in his heart.

He watched as Dackon dressed himself in gold, white, and red: a king, almost, lacking only the crown. Then, without a further glance in Lucah's direction, Dackon unlocked and opened the cabin door.

Sunlight streamed in, haloing his captain like a blood-streaked god.

A chorus of noise flooded through: boisterous laughter and the clashing of bones and shields and swords. They called to Lucah's soul, like the strings on his heart were pulled taut.

Dackon left.

The door shut behind him, and Lucah was bathed in shadows and solemnity and silence once more.

As the blood on his lips dried, his mind's fog fading, his thoughts grew to a crescendo: a cacophony of adoration and envy and *yearning*. Lucah needed Dackon with the entirety of his being.

His heart was empty without him.

And he would do everything he could to keep him.

Dackon must have had a reason to leave. Lucah knew that. He had responsibilities; he had the entirety of The Crimson Dead's crew to command. He would never leave Lucah's side unless out of necessity.

Dackon loved him. And Lucah loved Dackon in return.

As the fog faded into something numb, but tinged with copper, Lucah sat up. He brushed hands over bruises, bites, cuts, his memories nothing but fond. Then, he pushed the blanket aside and clambered out of bed, limbs wobbling. He did not quite fall.

He straightened, took a slow, deep breath, and then dressed himself in the clothes left out for him, the numbness fading away. It became something cooler, calmer, especially as he returned his hair to its ordinary white-webbed braid. His soul settled, his wounds grounding him, and serenity overtook whatever else remained.

His dagger slipped into its sheath.

And he, too, opened the cabin door and left.

Nothing was out of place.

His crew gambled, shouted, drank. They sliced their skin to sacrifice precious red to their god of Blood, though most were nothing more than Mundane. And none could sustain a man's immortality like Lucah.

His spine straightened, though his heart pounded like thunder. His lips twitched, especially as he did not allow his vain hatred to cross his features. He had a reputation to maintain, after all.

After a moment of scanning the deck, the realisation that Dackon was out of sight made Lucah's heart twinge. The urge to search almost overwhelmed him, though only momentarily. Reason returned. Shaking his head, he drummed fingers on his dagger, and crossed the deck.

"Did our captain give you a good time, eh, Lucah?"

"We could hear him fucking you from here!"

"Who would've thought a man like you would beg? Aren't you supposed to be prissy and perfect? Is Dackon's dick that good?"

"Maybe I need a taste of that."

Lucah's glare snapped onto Lyria, lounging in her merriment. She grinned, winked, and then returned to her games as if what she had said only irritated him, as if he did not wish to reach into her flesh and pluck out each of her bones. He would lick them clean of blood.

Lucah shook his head, loose strands slipping from its braid. He could find better targets to take out his fury on, targets Dackon would care less about careless slaying. He paused.

A target.

He had no need to search. Someone already awaited punishment, someone wholly and utterly deserving of it.

Lucah turned, laying eyes on the sea to his left. Just between Blodrik of Blood and Beake of Beasts, they were right in the middle of a red-tinged sea, stinking of sea-salt and rot. The blood had been spilling for millennia, and would for millennia to come.

The thought set Lucah's mind alight, but that was not his focus.

He strode to the edge of the ship, looking over slowly, cautiously, and his gaze fixed on a shimmering blue shape, far lighter than the dark, dark water. It almost seemed to glow, and it *certainly* seemed to beckon, beckon, beckon for Lucah to jump.

He did not.

Instead, he bent down and carefully removed his shoes, and then his socks. He tucked cloth into leather, and placed them beside Herrin, who he was sure was trustworthy enough not to toss them overboard. Then, with the graceful arc of a leaping fish, Lucah dove into the water.

He was submerged immediately, finding himself in the darker, bluer waves below the layer of blood. It pressed in on him – a magic not his own – and the instinctual panic set in before reason could return to his mind. He squirmed, ready to swim back up, before a hand caught his wrist from behind, one with slimy, webbed fingers.

Lucah was spun. Before he could think, a pair of lips smashed against his, sending a bubble between his teeth and down his throat.

He yanked himself away, taking a panting breath as his vision cleared and nerves relaxed like stormless waves. The kiss always startled him, but its magic was invaluable.

Ocellia cackled, bubbles spilling through her lips. Her narrow black eyes were alight with amusement, almost glowing, as her dark skin and darker curls blended in with the shadows of the water. Her cerulean tail, fins, and gills shimmered as if bioluminescent.

Her magic carried them easily alongside the ship.

She grinned with spiky teeth. "Did I scare you?" she squealed, darting all around, making his head spin. "Did I? Did I? Did I?"

Lucah glared. "No, you did not."

Ocellia cackled even louder, her tail swishing back and forth. "I did! Oh, silly Lu. I would never hurt you!" Her grin sharpened. "I'd have to move ships. And I love Dackon too, too much!"

Lucah's heart panged with a furious envy, though he knew what she meant. "Good," he spat. He did his best to straighten his spine, but it was difficult to do so whilst paddling and pushed by the waves. "Is our prisoner in a similar state?"

Instead of answering, Ocellia shot towards him, grabbed him by the wrist with bony fingers, and tugged him deeper underwater, to where those on the ship would never be able to see them. They followed a chain protruding from the bottom of

The Crimson Dead, though there was no anchor at the end.

What there was, when they reached it, was a cage. It was barely big enough for a person, and ever-dragged by this ship, never to see the light of day again, though the chain was speckled with Ocellia's hand-crafted lights. Fishbones and sea-glass reshaped into stars.

A woman, barely older than Ocellia, was curled in on herself, hiding lavender eyes behind brown hands, as if that would do anything to protect her. At just the sight of her, Ocellia released Lucah, and pressed both hands to the thick metal bars. She giggled like a madwoman.

"Are you gonna tell us your name yet, little human, or are you gonna keep screaming for your sister?" Ocellia knocked her head against one of the bars, hard enough that *Lucah* flinched, though she did not.

The prisoner curled in on herself, hiding her every precious feature and remaining as silent as a mourning corpse.

Lucah's lips twisted into a scowl.

He swam closer, grabbing a pair of bars even cooler than the water that cradled them. "What was a *human* doing with such powerful potions? Who did you steal them from?"

No answer came.

Lucah's fury rose.

He leant in, though he could not fit his face through the gaps, nor would he try to. His eyes darted over every inch of their captive: her ragged clothes, carefully stitched; her patchwork bag; her sheathed knife; the belt that had once held four potions of invisibility.

"Silly human!" Ocellia sang, sweet and melodic. "You didn't even take a sip! You could've hidden from us, right in front of our noses, and we never-never-never would've found you! But you don't know what you took, do you?"

"She's a human. That should be indicative enough."

Ocellia gave a spluttering giggle, giving Lucah a look of delight that had him rolling his eyes. He tuned out her repetitive rambles, hardly saying anything at all, and turned back to their captive.

"Do you have anything else of use to us?" he asked, words slow and almost gentle, had they not been tinged with cruelty. A familiar taste on a tongue always coated with someone else's blood. "Another potion? A cursed jewel? A hidden trinket?"

The prisoner did not spill a word, but she did shake her head. And though Lucah's magic had nothing to do with Truth, he was certain of her bitter veracity. He ran his tongue over his teeth.

Not enough. She had not earned the right to live, not in Lucah's eyes, not when she was as useless as seafoam-sword.

Lucah turned to Ocellia, whose babbling had turned into music.

"Open the cage," he said.

The babbles ceased. Ocellia blinked with those shadowed eyes, before her face split into another grin. She let out a giggle that sent bubbles shooting from her lips. "Did Captain give that order?"

Lucah quirked an eyebrow. "As his first mate, I have the power to order you, too."

The giggles became manic and wild. "Funny! Funny, funny, funny Lu. He's got you wrapped around his finger. Or maybe you have him wrapped around your throat."

She reached out, jabbing his scarred neck with a pointed nail. He snarled, kicking himself away, but she twisted her wrist. The water dragged her right back to him, so close they were nose-to-nose. She stared, bared her teeth, and then poked his forehead.

"You don't have any more power than I do, Lucah." Ocellia smiled, tilting her head. "Or any less."

The first was a familiar sentiment. He had heard it all before: from family, friends. The people he had left behind.

Lucah knew they were wrong.

But the latter statement bemused him, and he scowled with unhidden rage. "What do you mean?" he demanded.

Ocellia's pearly teeth were on display, though they were rarely hidden away, even when she was docile. "You don't have to stay," she sang. "If you want a lover who loves you, you can always *leave*. You have no power here, but you could every-

every-everywhere! We could see the world, Lu! We could reach the edges of Ungode, and bite everyone we see along the way. Don't you want that?"

Lucah gave a cold, hard stare. "You may leave, if you wish to," he said, icy and flat. "But I will follow my captain, because he is my everything, and because I am his everything, too."

Ocellia cackled, shaking her head. "Silly, silly Lu."

"Ocellia, I am unafraid to cut you."

"Oh, I'm sure you are! But we're in water, Lu-Lu."

Lucah's heart jolted as the water grabbed his braid, yanking on it and exposing his throat. Ocellia's tongue flicked, like she wished to lick the scars on his skin, but she did not. Instead, she rose and stared right into his eyes, like the blood of a human against the powers of the sea.

She made it impossible to forget the inhumanity of followers of Water, and how dangerous they could be.

But Lucah was dangerous, too. He glared.

Ocellia laughed once more and released him, the tension breaking like an unfixed puzzle. "You're so funny, Lu!" She clapped her hands together. "I'm not leaving, too. You're just too much fun!"

Lucah's glare sharpened. It only made her giggle again.

Finally, after his glower lost its fire, his eyes closed. He massaged the bridge of his nose, before he decided to push his anger onto something far more productive, more *interesting.*

His eyes fixated on the caged woman, who had not stopped trembling. Her nails were chewed like there had been nothing else to gnaw on, leaving bloodied marks on every finger.

She was powerless. She was human. She hardly mattered at all.

Lucah did not know why, but that, more than anything, made his fury bubble and spread, like mould on a festering corpse. His mind flicked to his dagger, as did both of his hands.

"If you're not going to be of any use," he spat, "then you might as well fill our stomachs with flesh."

* * *

Lucah paid little attention to the gathering beside him.

Coins and cards were scattered across the table he leant against, but he was not one of the players, nor was he nearly so intoxicated. His flask was still half-full of beast-blood wine, and his eyes were firmly fixed on the cabin door. Locked.

Locked, and yet he was outside.

He was outside, on the deck, amongst the uncouth pirates he so despised, as they spat curses and liquor that hit his twitching jaw. He was outside, and he was *not with Dackon.*

His fingers drummed on the table, between tossed dice that narrowly missed his knuckles, and his other hand gripped his flask so tightly that the skin was white. His eyes did not move.

Dackon. Dackon. Dackon.

He mouthed the name, again and again and again, though he was already oh-so accustomed to tasting it on his tongue.

"You're getting kinda pathetic, aren't you, Lu?"

Lucah jolted, his head snapping to the source of the voice.

A bubbling bed of water floated just above the sea, right beside the docked ship. There lay Ocellia, with her bare chest and shimmering scales and look of sweet, sweet mockery.

Lucah scowled, slamming his flask onto the table, jolting the cards, though the inebriated gamblers hardly noticed. "Excuse me? Who are you to call *me* pathetic?"

Ocellia smiled, shaking her head as if exasperated. "Silly, silly Lu."

Lucah's snarl exposed the teeth that would rip through her throat, if the need arose. But she simply giggled and displayed her shark-like teeth, reminding him of her carnivorous diet. Even the fruit she occasionally indulged in, between fish torn apart by slimy claws, stained her mouth like *she* was the blood-drinker.

She stank of violence, but not the fresh-bloodied kind Lucah was drawn to. She was salted and rotten.

Lucah almost leapt at her, but came to his senses before he even twitched. He smoothed over his features, squeezed his flask, and then took a sip. It burned his throat.

"Ocellia," he said, calm. "You're going to get yourself killed."

"Am I?"

"Most certainly."

"How? How are you going to do it?"

Lucah raised an eyebrow. "Is this a challenge?"

Ocellia's eyes widened, alight with a newfound delight. "Oh! Oh, oh, oh! Are you *actually* going to fight me, Lu?"

Her excitement curdled his meagre rations. "A follower of Water can never be killed amongst the waves, not unless matched by someone of equal power, blessed by the very same god," Lucah said. "And you could never journey far from the water, even with that bubble you travel with. It would kill you. That's hardly an equal match."

"Is that a no?"

Lucah rolled his eyes, finally looking away. But as he lifted his flask to his lips once more, poised to take a swig, the cabin's door finally opened. He choked on nothing, and Ocellia cackled.

Lucah could not look at her. He rose, abandoning his flask to spill across the table, ignoring the drunken protests that followed. He strode across the deck, and reached Dackon just as he closed the door behind him, locking it with a click.

Dackon turned, raising an eyebrow. "Do you need something?"

Cold.

Lucah's heart stuttered. But he did not allow

that to overwhelm him. Instead, he straightened his spine as if anything less would betray the man he worshipped more than anything. He clasped his hands in front of his stomach. "Is there anything you need from me, captain?"

Dackon stared: silent and almost considering, filling the air with nothing but Lucah's heartbeat and breaths.

"No," Dackon finally said. "I'm going to take a walk."

Lucah leant in on the tips of his toes. "May I accompany you?"

"No."

There was not an ounce of hesitation, not a glimpse of guilt on Dackon's face. He simply looked past Lucah, as if he meant nothing at all, and began to walk away. Lucah blinked, a little startled, before he turned and trailed after him, scurrying like a puppy.

"What are your orders?" he asked, desperate and wobbly, as if the sea had never once been his home. "What do I—"

"Stay on the ship. Make sure nobody drowns."

And with that, without even a glance back over his shoulder, Dackon stepped from the ship, onto the docks, and strode away, into the town of rickety red buildings, puddles of crimson, and streets scattered with blood-guzzling rodents, who did not ask so nicely as Dackon did.

Lucah could not move until he was completely out of sight, until there was no crimson and gold to hold his gaze.

He could hardly breathe, even then.

"Are you going to cry, Lu?"

Lucah's head snapped to Ocellia, and he glared with the venom that had never once made her flinch. She simply tilted her head, lounging in the bubble of water that floated above the deck.

"He'll return," Lucah said.

"Oh, I'm sure." Ocellia paused. "Or he won't."

She flopped onto her back, tail flicking and spraying water into Lucah's face. The taste almost made him gag, but he refused to, instead scowling and wiping it away with a silky sleeve. Ocellia flicked once more, and Lucah swiftly yanked his dagger from its sheath. He whipped it through the air, and a hand formed of water caught it before it could pierce Ocellia's throat.

For a moment, Lucah and Ocellia were engulfed by silence, though surrounded by noise. And then Ocellia fell into cackles. She cackled like nothing else had ever filled her with quite so much glee.

The water reached out and dropped the dagger into Lucah's palm. A silent glower settled on his face, and he tucked it back into his sheath.

"Lu," Ocellia sang. "Do you want to do something fun?"

"I am not leaving Dackon's side."

Ocellia waved her hand dismissively. "Yes, yes." She leant in. "But I don't mean forever and ever and ever, Lu! I mean... don't you want to see where Dackon's going?"

Heart jolting, Lucah's eyes snapped to where he had last seen his captain, before he had turned a corner and disappeared from sight. He could almost make out his silhouette, but even Lucah knew he had an overactive imagination. He swallowed.

"What are you proposing?"

Ocellia squealed, flapping her hands, and Lucah snapped to glare at her once more. Her face was as entertained as it always was, alight with a lively delight. In an instant, her lips were beside his ear.

In an uncharacteristic display of subtlety, she whispered, "we can still *disappear*, you know? For just a moment."

Lucah's brow furrowed, bewilderment forming on his lips, twisting into frustration, before it hit him. The potions. His gaze snapped to the cabin's door, and then returned to Ocellia.

She waggled her eyebrows. "Come *on*," she said. "You cannot tell me you don't wish to follow him. I see it in your eyes, Lu!"

Lucah's jaw tensed.

Ocellia's black eyes had never been brighter. They glimmered like moonlight on a shard of obsidian, like starlight on the infinite sea. They lured Lucah in, like every tale told by sailors of the dangers of the deep. The dangers of followers of Water.

There were more of them than any other kind, of course. And they could be *anywhere.*

Ungode was flat, with an island for every magic,

at least one kingdom for each. They were nestled in seven great seas, and all cradled by an ocean that did not end. Infinite in every direction. But the further one travelled from the centre, the deadlier it became.

No one knew what was at the edges, if such a thing even existed. All that was known was that it was a death sentence.

And something in Ocellia's eyes made Lucah certain that those of her magic held a power unknown and a wisdom unfathomable. She was luring him to something; the logical part of his mind knew that.

But he wanted it oh-so desperately.

"I'm going to fetch the potions."

Ocellia brightened like an opening sea-flower, that shadowed expression replaced by another of delight. She clapped her hands together, sitting up. Her tail sprayed water across the deck.

"Oh, Lu! I knew this'd be a good day! Quickly, quickly, quickly!"

She made an exaggerated shooing gesture, and Lucah found himself incapable of resisting. He hurried to the cabin door, and fished the spare key from where it always sat in the depths of his pocket, just opposite his dagger. Without a glance to the eyes that were on him, he unlocked the door, marching inside as if confident.

He closed the door behind him.

He found the potions within moments, tucked away in the first drawer he peered into – the first that was unlocked. The rest almost-literally *called* to him. But Lucah knew there was no chance of finding whatever Dackon wished not to share, nor did he wish to anger him.

As Lucah had seen hundreds of times, constellation-like scars speckled Dackon's torso and limbs. Tales of violent conquests sprung to mind, but Dackon had hardly revealed any of them to Lucah.

Secrets filled him to his core.

Something heavy settled in Lucah's stomach, like he had swallowed a dozen coins, but he pushed the feeling aside. He gathered two potions, fastened them to his belt, and scurried from the room as quickly as he could. He managed to lock the door behind him, though only just.

Lucah did not look at any who watched, even as they mocked him. Most grew bored within moments. A fickle bunch.

"What are you going to do with your water?" asked Lucah once he had returned to Ocellia's side. Her excitement had only grown in their minutes apart. "Don't you need it?"

Ocellia giggled into her palm. "I'll keep just enough to cover my gills. Potions are fickle, you know! My water-bed won't be subtle enough, and I can't exactly grow legs!" Her giggles morphed into cackles. "You're a strong man, aren't you, Lu? Carry me."

Lucah's brow furrowed. "You're... larger than I am."

"Aww. Are you a weakling?"

"Nothing of the sort." Despite his words, he eyed her warily. She was more muscular than he was, though they were close to the same height. "I'm sure I can manage it."

When Ocellia's grin returned, her teeth were twice as sharp.

✳ ✳ ✳

It had been strangely easy to track Dackon, which Lucah supposed was because no one else would dare to, or because Ocellia was eerily proficient at it. Like a dog that had never known anything but how to track, how to beg, and how to bite.

"Left," she hissed into Lucah's ear, her breath like raw fish.

He jolted, almost dropping her, but veered left.

Ocellia lounged in his arms like he was her water-bed, though he half-wished he was, instead, her casket. The urge to drop her almost overwhelmed him, especially with the difficulties of carrying someone as invisible as he was, but he suppressed it.

She giggled as he held her closer, dripping red-tinged water down his clothes – the droplets only visible, to his eyes, when they became as much a part of him as his boots.

"How do you know this?" Lucah hissed, darting across a bridge as quickly as he could, ignoring its rickety planks. The metallic scent of the stream below dried his throat. "How could you possibly—"

"I have a much better nose than you, Lu-Lu!" came Ocellia's shrill voice, as unsubtle as could be. "And Dackon always smells so bloody. Just like you, but even-even-even stronger!"

Despite the truth of her statement, Lucah scowled.

Ocellia's hand danced up his arm, her fingers like wet knives, before squeezing his bicep. "You're still my favourite, Lu," she whispered as if it were the sweetest of secrets.

Lucah rolled his eyes. "You should not disrespect our captain."

"Oh, hush. I only do it with you!"

"Now, that I know is a lie."

Ocellia blew a raspberry, and foul-smelling spittle sprayed from her tongue, splattering across his cheek. She giggled as if she could see the disgust on his face. "Right!" she called.

Lucah turned, lips forming his next words, mind spiralling to keep up, before he caught sight of it.

A waterfall of scarlet hair. A long cloak, embroidered with strands of gold. And a pair of white hands, drumming fingers against a tavern's outside table. Its rings matched Lucah's, though they were far more extravagant than the one he so often found himself watching.

Lucah's heart stopped.

Those features were carved from marble, as if they were not of this world. Dackon was a great, ethereal creature. His lips left bruises where Lucah most wished for them, his nails scraping so hard they drew blood. No one could make Lucah writhe and whine like Dackon could.

He did not realise he had frozen until Ocellia's hand returned to his bicep, squeezing with a force that made him bite his tongue.

She hummed, musing. "Who could he be waiting for, I wonder?"

"Silence."

"Hmm?"

"*Silence*," Lucah hissed. "He might hear us."

Ocellia paused, neither whispering nor wriggling, though only for a bittersweet moment. When she resumed, her lowered voice took on a teasing tint. "You're on board with this plan now, huh?"

"Ocellia, stop talking."

"Why? Nothing's happening yet—"

A woman passed Dackon's table and something slipped from her palm, landing right between his drumming fingers. She said nothing, did nothing more, did not even *acknowledge* him, and simply began to whistle, stuffing her hands into her pockets as she wandered away.

Dackon stared at whatever it was for a few moments, something cool and contemplative on his face. As he watched it, Lucah took a tentative step forward, before yelping as Ocellia pinched his arm.

"We don't want to be caught, do we, Lu-Lu?"

Lucah pressed his lips together, but remained where he was. He could see Dackon – could read his features clearly, could taste the blood on his teeth – but he could not see what his captain was watching.

That was, until Dackon reached out and picked it up.

A shard of glass, glinting in sunlight like a golden mirror.

He raised it, and then scowled. "What are you doing?"

Lucah's heart stopped. Had he seen right through the invisibility?

Ocellia froze, too, but Dackon did not look their way. There was nothing on his face but a growing irritation: a curl to his lip, a venom in his eyes. And it was certainly not aimed at them. He gave no indication that he had seen the two on the verge of *treason*.

That did not calm Lucah's soul.

And the cackles that came from that shard, echoing like no other sound mattered, made him bare his teeth.

"Dackon!" came the melodious call of a woman unknown. "Have you grown since I last saw you?"

There were people scattered around the tavern's outside tables, and several found their gazes drawn to Dackon and his shard. Though some stares lingered, the rest of the townsfolk returned to their mugs and meals within moments. Their blades pulled droplets of blood from sweat-stained skin, and then dropped them into strips of raw fish and spiced rum. They gobbled them up with a sugar-sweet delight.

For a kingdom of rampant violence and poverty – always at war with someone, as if it was their true calling – Blodrik was rich with all that mattered: those who wished for nothing more than to be victims.

The only follower of Blood who did not was Dackon.

His lips twitched. "You haven't."

"Aww, are you angry? Would a good fuck calm you down?"

Ocellia giggled, pinching Lucah's arm again. He barely felt it.

"My pet satisfies me enough," Dackon said, leaning back in his chair and balancing his empty hand on his sword's hilt, decorated with rubies and spiderwebs. "Do you need something, V?"

A term of endearment?

The cackle returned, tripled in size, like what Dackon had said was the height of hilarity. "Oh, it's been so long since I heard that little nickname. Too long, I'd say."

"And yet you have not come to visit me in person?" Dackon's voice was low, and thick with something Lucah could not discern.

"What would you do if I did? Would you try to kill me again?"

"I'm considering it."

"Ha! I'm sure you are. But what if I've been

considering it, too?"

"You're not the type."

"Am I not?"

Dackon shifted on the spot. For a moment, it looked as if he were about to stand, but instead he crossed one leg over the other, adjusting his cloak. He cast a glance over the people closest to him, feasting on blood and flesh with the enthusiasm of an infant at a breast.

He, of course, could not see Lucah and Ocellia.

Her tail dripped more reddish water onto his boots, staining them further. Her breaths were quick, but soft, like her nerves were as alight as a shooting star: bright, but fleeting. Lucah almost wished to see her face, to see what she thought of all this.

Who was this woman, who Lucah knew nothing of, nothing more than what had just been said aloud?

"We haven't spoken in years, V. And yet you only contact me now?"

Silence.

Dackon's jaw twitched. "V?"

A sigh, followed by laughter. "You've always been my favourite, Dackon." The voice grew slow: a tease that bordered on mockery. "I'm docked in Blodrik, too. Come find my ship. It's exactly how you remember it, especially my cabin."

Lucah breathed through clenched teeth, his fury building like blood about to burst from his veins. And, for a moment, Ocellia made not a sound, either. Then, she giggled, though it was smothered by her hand.

He would have smacked her, had he not had her in his arms. And he could not drop her, either, not when she already knew too much.

But what *did* they know?

It was something Dackon wished not to share, that much was obvious. A tale from his past, an old ally returned. But why would he keep such a secret from Lucah? What even *was* this secret?

Lucah's stomach churned, his hands quivering, his fury continuing to build. Who was this woman? Who was she to talk to Dackon like that, when he was *Lucah's*?

Dackon belonged to nobody else.

Lucah swallowed the vile curses that wished to fall from his teeth.

"I'll be there in an hour," Dackon finally said, his irritation oozing from his lips like sap. "Does The Everdrowned look the same?"

"Oh, you'll recognise it, Dackon. It'll be just like coming home."

Dackon let out a huff of laughter, head tilting back and exposing the pristine column of his throat. "Sure," he drawled, as sarcastic as sailors loved to be. "Just like coming home."

And, with that, he raised the shard of glass, giving Lucah a glimpse of gold, before he let go. It shattered against the table, but Dackon did nothing more than sweep aside the remains and stand. The glass crunched under his boots, and, without even a look back over his shoulder, he walked off.

Lucah began to follow, but that was when he caught sight of Ocellia, lounging in his invisible arms. He yelped, and, instinctively, ducked into the nearest alleyway.

She and her water slipped from his grip, all falling to the ground with a splash and a thud. For a moment, she flopped like a half-dead fish, making his anxiety spike as she tried desperately to breathe, before she gathered her senses and flicked her wrist. The water rose, making a bubble, and it wrapped around her face and gills like a helmet.

She sighed, relieved – eyes closing briefly – before she looked Lucah over. He was visible now, too, it seemed.

His heart pounded.

And, for a few moments, the pair breathed heavily.

Then, finally, Ocellia laughed. She flopped onto her back, arms splayed like a rot-reeking starfish. "Gods! That was *hilarious*." She grinned up at Lucah. "Isn't that hilarious? He's found a *replacement* for you. A pretty lady who knows more about him than you do."

The knife was in Lucah's hand before he could think. And it was at Ocellia's throat before he came to his senses.

For a split second, her eyes went wide. Then, she seemed to see something on his face that *screamed* that he could not go through with it, as she relaxed once more. She raised her hand, placing one finger on the blade, and pushed it aside. It only left the littlest red stain on her skin: a blooming rose, though so tiny she likely did not notice it.

And yet, Lucah fixated on it.

Ocellia blew a kiss, and a bubble of water hit him right between the eyes, knocking him from his daze. He stumbled back a few steps.

"Ocellia, you—you—"

The words fled from Lucah's throat, as did his every remaining breath. He almost would have believed it to have been Ocellia's doing, at least from the look on her face, had he not known for certain that it was not one of her abilities.

Through trembling fingers, the knife slipped from Lucah's grip.

Ocellia leant back on both hands, raising her eyebrows in a manner both curious and mocking. "Are you all right, Lu?"

Lucah panted, falling against the alleyway's wall, scraping his fingers on crumbling bricks. Flakes of dried blood covered his skin. Blodrik was filled with sacrifices aplenty.

Sacrifices to the god who would otherwise destroy them.

Stumbling back with quick, heavy breaths, Lucah turned. And as a man passed him by, whistling a tune with wine on his lips, Lucah grabbed him by the back of his shirt. He yanked him into the alleyway, spun him, and grabbed his knife from the ground in a quick, practised motion. As natural as breathing.

Before the man could question him, the blade was buried to the hilt in his stomach. He screamed, as did Lucah, though Lucah's was out of a primal, animalistic *fury*.

The knife was yanked out with a sickening squelch, painting Lucah's face and tongue with sugar-sweet crimson. A delicacy like no other. It tore through the stranger's skin, spilling guts from the jagged hole in his belly. He licked his lips, and aimed for the heart next.

Lucah tossed him to the ground, flipping his knife, and screamed again as he straddled the waist of the near-corpse. The blood set his nerves alight, filling him with strength and speed unmatched.

He aimed for the throat, and he stabbed and he stabbed and he stabbed until the head was no longer connected to the body.

And then he slid from the corpse, rolled onto his back, and allowed the knife to slip from his grip. With panting breaths, he closed his eyes, limbs splayed like ropes would yank them from his torso.

He was vulnerable to attack, especially in a kingdom such as this, but every splatter of blood across his skin made his heart sing.

Lucah could, finally, breathe.

His aches slipped away, though there was too much power in his body, all wishing to flee *somehow*. He could take on an army.

Silence.

No one came to the victim's rescue, though dozens must have heard the screams.

* * *

Lucah paced back and forth. His heavy footsteps – though louder than his pounding heart – should have left indents in the floor. Everyone on or below deck could certainly hear them. He paced anyway.

They had heard far worse.

And this, at most, would make them *laugh*.

Lucah ran his tongue over his teeth, each so pointed and rough that his lips had been scarred since childhood. Dackon loved to bite and tear them, too, scraps of flesh split by sharkish fangs.

Lucah had always said yes. And he had always loved every moment of it, had never held even an ounce of regret.

Did that mean anything? He hoped so.

The doorhandle turned, and Lucah inhaled sharply, halting so suddenly he stumbled. For a moment, he refused to even *breathe*, before he turned and met Dackon's gaze.

Dackon did not say a word.

Lucah's stomach dropped. "Captain." He clasped his hands behind his back. "How was your... excursion?"

A moment passed. Two. Three.

Dackon's shoulders relaxed. Miniscule. Identifiable only by someone who had watched him for almost a decade, eyes on a statue hand-carved by the divine. Lucah's shoulders relaxed, too.

"It was fine," Dackon said, as flat as a blade. "If you'll excuse me, Lucah, I have things to attend to."

"Things... that I can assist with?"

"That won't be necessary." Dackon pushed past him, crossing the cabin with long strides and coming to a halt beside his chair. He sat on the crimson cushion, and did not spare Lucah another glance.

Silence.

Lucah swallowed. "But... could I?"

Dackon stilled. He almost could have been carved from marble. It was as if he had no need to breathe, though only for a moment. Then, he turned to Lucah, and met his eyes with a gaze as sharp as his teeth.

Another silence overcame them, filled only with the distant shouts of pirates below the stars, haloed by the constellation of Blodrik that looked much alike a splatter on a cloak. A hero's descent into bloodlust.

Or so Lucah had been told.

Dackon stood. He crossed the room, and caught Lucah's chin between his fingers. He leant down, and Lucah instinctively rose onto his tiptoes. His eyelids were moments from slipping shut.

But Dackon did not kiss him. Instead, he turned Lucah's head from side-to-side. Slow. Careful.

Lucah found himself almost more bewildered

than anything else, though butterflies still fluttered through every part of his cavernous belly and chest. A bittersweet yearning filled his soul.

Dackon furrowed his brow. "Has something upset you, pet?"

Taking a quivering breath, Lucah leant in. "Nothing at all."

There was a beat.

Dackon's other hand rose, and gloved fingertips brushed Lucah's cheek. The touch was gentle, but held the implicit knowledge that he had so much more strength lingering in his bones. Dackon could do anything he liked, and no one on The Crimson Dead would ever be able to stop him. And yet, each remained loyal to the other.

Lucah swallowed, thick and unsteady, but his fear intermingled with an overwhelming warmth in his belly. He wished to melt into Dackon's arms, was only moments from doing so.

"Pet?" Dackon's grip tightened. "What aren't you telling me?"

A sharp inhale. "Nothing, captain."

"Lucah?"

"I don't…" He averted his gaze.

"Lucah."

His chin was squeezed – nails digging in, even through white silk – and he was forced to meet Dackon's eyes once more. Nothing could ever have been so tantalising, so sweet on the tip of his tongue.

Dackon leant in, an aroma of blood slipping

from his teeth. His jaw twitched, eyes narrowed, and he pulled Lucah in closer.

"What do you know?"

"Excuse me?"

"What do you know, Lucah?"

"Nothing, captain," Lucah began to babble, focused on nothing but that blood-filled gaze. "It was just... Ocellia. She caught sight of something. And she told me of it." His mind raced, though far from the tremulous pace of his heart.

Dackon's narrowing eyes did nothing to help, only worsening his terror and lust and wish to do nothing more than drop to his knees and *obey.* There was something strangely comforting about that thought, but Lucah pushed the feeling aside.

"What did she see?" Dackon asked. Slow. Cold.

Lucah's heart jumped, before pounding violently against the bars of his ribcage. "Just..." He scrambled to find the right words: the words that would not get them slaughtered on the spot. "Another ship. She saw you on another ship, and thought you and the captain were... close. She made a handful of unsavoury comments."

Dackon stared.

For a few seconds – for almost a *minute*, perhaps even two – he was utterly immovable. And then he let go. He turned, waving his hand.

"Ignore the rumours," Dackon said. "That captain and I were allies once upon a time, and that's all there is to it. I didn't stick around for long. You may go now, pet, if that was all she saw."

Lucah breathed a sigh of relief. "Oh. That's... good."

Dackon sat at his desk, producing a key from one of his pockets, and unlocked the drawer just above where only two potions remained.

As Lucah's heart lurched, his hand jerked in unison.

But Dackon did not notice. Instead, he retrieved a paper, a quill, and an engraved pot of ink. He began to write in a cursive dialect Lucah could not quite pinpoint. A mystery forever unrevealed.

Lucah could not focus on that.

If Dackon were to discover the missing potions, who would he kill in his efforts to recover the truth? How long would it take until the culprit was found? How long would it take until Dackon killed them?

Lucah wished to vomit. He wished to scream. He wished to beg, though Dackon no longer thought he needed to.

Dackon *trusted* him. Did Lucah deserve it?

Guilt mingled with Lucah's fear. He thought he really would vomit.

Dackon looked to him once more, and raised a single eyebrow, sitting on the border of condescension. "Do you need something?"

Lucah opened his mouth, tried to speak, but no word emerged. Dackon continue to stare, expectant, yet almost bored. Lucah had disappointed him, though there was no fury, and it was impossible to navigate such a thing.

Swallowing, Lucah shifted his weight from one foot to the other, hands clasped together. "May I... kiss you, captain?"

He had rarely been the one to ask.

Dackon was just as startled as Lucah, who had not expected those to be the words to slip from his lips. But he could not rescind the offer, nor could he deny that it was what he wanted more than anything.

For a moment, Dackon stared, before he leant back in his chair. He crossed his arms. "Have you earned it?"

Lucah shivered, and then stood straighter. "I've done everything you've ever asked me to." Lie. "I've never been unfaithful, not in any sense." Lie. "And I just..." He paused. "I want to ensure you're not going to leave us. We're *nothing* without you, captain."

"You mean *you're* nothing, right?"

Lucah swallowed. "Yes, I do."

Silence.

Dackon looked him over, just the slightest tilt of his head. Then, he stood. He strode over to Lucah, caught him by the chin once again, and tugged him into a kiss. When their lips collided, it was rough – almost *violent* – but Lucah melted like he was being handled with utmost adoration and care.

He kissed back.

His hands balled the front of Dackon's shirt, and he allowed the entirety of his weight to be pressed against his captain. If Dackon moved at all, if he pulled away for any reason, then Lucah would fall. He was almost certain he would never rise again.

But Lucah did not care.

The only thing that filled his blood-and-lust mind was *Dackon, Dackon, Dackon.* And that only further overwhelmed him as Dackon plucked him from the floor and took him to bed.

❊ ❊ ❊

Lucah awoke alone.

The bed was cold, like a dip in an ice-curdling sea, and Lucah's bare flesh was covered with prickly hairs. He shivered, curling in on himself, before he pushed the blankets aside. Once he could see himself entirely, he found pretty bruises covering his chest and clambering his throat, though those stretched out of his line of sight.

Reaching up, he ran his fingers over the older scars that speckled his throat, and then the newest one: now as cool as the rest of him. He shivered, but pushed his longing aside and climbed out of bed.

His limbs shook when his feet hit the floor, but he only wobbled for a moment or two, before he hurried to dress himself. By the time he was covered and decorated and out of the door, he had regained his usual composure, and adjusted quickly to the early-morning sun, though its rays made his heart even colder.

Lucah swallowed the blood on his tongue.

He adjusted his waistcoat, then the web in his hair, before, finally, he ran his fingers over his scarred throat once more. His tongue lingered on his teeth, pressing down until the metallic taste returned.

It was almost like Dackon's blood remained on his tongue, but they had never tasted quite the same.

He scanned the deck.

Herrin raised two fingers, saluting with a lazy half-smile, as Lyria called her usual rampant mockery. The rest of the crew, though Lucah was above them all, ignored him, mostly.

Lucah's stomach churned. He decided not to think about them.

Ocellia was nowhere in sight, and Lucah found himself frowning, his brow furrowing. His fingers found their way onto the dagger's hilt, though he did not yet make a move to unsheathe it. Even as he wandered left and peered over the side of the ship, he caught no glimpse of her iridescent tail in the shallow water by the docks.

Fishbones and cracked skulls were dotted through the waves, mingling with seaweed and blood, giving the impression that she had been there *recently*, but not anymore. That almost frightened him.

Lucah turned around, scanning the deck and the docks once more, but he found nothing. Sailors were dotted all around, but the corpse-rot on their clothes did nothing more than turn his stomach. There was no one akin to an ally in sight: begrudged or not.

Wherever Ocellia was, she was out of reach, but he could almost hear her whispers in his ear. *Dackon was not there, either. And he seldom went below deck.* Had he returned to The Everdrowned?

Lucah's heart raced.

Had Dackon *abandoned* him?

Lucah grabbed the side of the ship before he could collapse, before his heart could shoot from his chest and spray everything with sweet scarlet. No one cared. Lucah's breaths became quick, heavy, erratic, especially as his chest tightened like his lungs were squeezed.

No one spared him more than a glance and a chuckle.

Lucah needed to find Dackon.

That thought was all that echoed through his empty mind and cavernous heart. He needed to find Dackon, more than he had ever needed anything before.

Lucah needed to bring Dackon home. He needed to kiss him and fuck him and worship him until Dackon never left his side again.

Lucah was back in the cabin before he could even begin to form his plan. He was tucking the third and fourth invisibility potions into a bag as the ideas began to swirl in his skull. And he was leaving the ship once he knew *exactly* what he was going to do next.

The second set of docks were easily reached. They were in a neighbouring town, of course, but Lucah was no stranger to wandering the streets of Blodrik. He was no stranger to dodging bloated corpses and bloodied children and humans begging to be put out of their misery.

Perhaps, once upon a time, Lucah would have given in to their demands. But, now, he ignored those who begged for death, and stomped on the hands of those who reached for him.

The wind carried screams, carried prayers, carried whispers.

And, soon, the wind carried the returning aroma of sea salt, mingling with copper on his tongue.

Lucah ducked behind a house the moment another set of ships came into sight, their masts and sails peeking over and around dark, rickety buildings. His hand dipped into his bag, fingers closing around the cool, damp neck of the bottle. He uncorked it carefully, tossed the cork aside, before he raised the potion to his lips.

He guzzled it, sweet and sticky, and then scrubbed at his mouth with his sleeve, embroidered to look like curling waves, with their threads half-dyed with blood. The taste lingered on his tongue, but that was hardly what occupied Lucah's mind.

Dackon. Dackon. Dackon.

Taking a breath, eyes slipping shut, he became but another part of the sky. He could identify the tears of Illusions, the salty base of Water, the hints of fallen clouds of Air. They overtook his every organ and limb, and every weapon and cloth he considered a part of himself, too.

Soon, he was invisible. Gone.

No one would ever know he was there.

The bottle shattered against the stone street.

With a slow caution and the furrow of his brow, Lucah stepped around the building, ensuring his footfalls were as silent as could be. He knew not what lurked on The Everdrowned, after all.

He followed a malodorous man, dressed in rags of carnation and jewellery of gold, his heavy footsteps masking Lucah's own. He was, predictably enough, stumbling over to the ship that stood out against the rest: great and towering, with sails of pure, unsullied gold.

It looked more ancient than even The Crimson Dead.

As the man reached the ship, before he could even step aboard, Lucah scurried around him, landing on the deck with light feet and a thunderous heart. His eyes darted around, drinking in his surroundings with the hunger of a dead man.

Dackon was nowhere in sight.

Neither was anyone who looked even a little like him. It seemed everyone aboard this ship was utterly of the Mundane: milk-scented and flesh-born, never cradled in the embrace of a god.

Human.

Lucah's nose wrinkled, but his stomach settled. He would be able to fight his way out, should the need arise. Despite that, he kept his hand on his knife, ready to be brandished at a moment's notice.

He surveyed the deck again, watching pirates load crates of supplies onto the ship, chattering like the crew he had always despised.

Where was Dackon?

He had to be on this ship. He *had* to be.

Where else would he be? Who else could have stolen him away?

Lucah's breaths turned to desperate pants, battling in his lungs to be the first to flee his throat. They burned as if aflame.

He knew Dackon better than he knew himself. And he *knew*, in his soul, that Dackon was here. But where?

Where? Where? Where?

Lucah's eyes fixed onto the gold-flecked cabin door, and something sour settled in his gut. He strode across the deck, dodging slumbering bodies – dead and alive – and shards of shattered glass, scattered cards, sharpened blades. A feather. A twig. They did not unsettle him nearly as much as the thought of his captain with another, with someone utterly, utterly unworthy of him.

Lucah was hardly worthy, either, but he would spend the rest of his life becoming the lover that Dackon deserved. His resolution turned to stone, and he reached the cabin door.

For a second, he reached out, instinctive, before

he snatched his hand back. He had to be *careful*. He did not know what lay beyond.

He cast a cautious glance back over his shoulder, and then down at his own body. No one was looking his way, and he was, it seemed, just as invisible as before.

A woman with dark braids was fixing a silver earring, fiddling with a blessed coin, unaware of who watched. A pair of teenagers fought with swords, encouraged by a gathering that stank of rum. A lanky man scribbled on stained paper, adjusting his glasses every few seconds.

Lucah turned back to the door. He leant in, slow, and pressed his ear to the warm wood. Muffled voices chattered beyond.

"Dackon," sang this vessel's captain. "Are you listening?"

"I am."

"Not very well, I must say. You've hardly responded at all!"

"If you said something of note, I would."

A laugh. No, a *cackle* was the more apt descriptor. "Oh, Dackon, you haven't changed a bit! But it really has been *far* too long. Isn't that funny? We haven't crossed paths in years, have hardly even been in the same kingdom, and yet we've found ourselves together once again, purely by coincidence!"

"I don't believe there is such a thing."

Breaths of desperation poured through Lucah's parted lips. Every time this woman spoke, a dagger pierced his heart. And every time Dackon responded, a violent sea churned in Lucah's gut. He swallowed the bile that clogged his throat.

With the laugh of a hyena, this madwoman further descended upon Dackon, as if she was digging her claws into his chest. "Oh, you and your superstitions!" Her voice was high and entertained: half an insult, half a tease. Who was she to speak to Dackon in such a manner? He was not hers. "Not everything is written in stone, Dackon, no matter what *old friends* made it seem."

"Get to the point, V, or I'm leaving.

Lucah breathed a sigh of relief.

Dackon was leaving; perhaps he may even fight his way out. Lucah would see this deck stained red, and all would return to how it should be. Dackon would come home; Lucah would return to his arms.

"Yes, yes, yes." There was a rustle of fabric, like hands over a silky coat. "I'll get to the point." A pause came, and then a chuckle. "Look, don't you miss how things used to be: us against the world? We lived aboard this ship, did nothing but sail and sing, and we were happy!"

"I don't regret leaving. And I don't miss what we had."

"Oh, you will."

A pause. Lucah held his breath.

"What happens if I say yes?" asked Dackon. "What then, V?"

Heart leaping into his throat, Lucah's legs failed.

He fell into the door: a thud that echoed across the deck, and likely into the captain's cabin, too. Many heads turned his way, though they could not see him.

He scrambled to his feet, thanking the gods he was still invisible. His hand found his dagger, and he yanked it from its sheath.

It buzzed with the need for blood.

He needed to kill her. He needed to get in there and stab her and *run* before Dackon caught him, before Dackon did something Lucah *knew* he would regret. He would, most certainly, regret it.

Dackon only ever hurt Lucah when he begged him to.

Lucah knew what he needed to do.

He raised his dagger, its curling grooves pressing into his fingertips, its splatters of blood travelling up the blade and over the handle and into his skin. It seeped through his flesh, fuelling him, making him *strong*. It was far unlike his power from blood freshly spilled, but it set his heart alight. Promises from his god pressed into his soul.

As he pulled back, Lucah found himself more certain of his choices than he had ever been before. His breaths quickened, his heart's pounding having grown to a cacophonous crescendo, before he embedded the knife in the door.

Dragging it down with all his strength, he tore through the wood, leaving behind a splintered, gaping hole. Through it, he caught a glimpse of red hair and golden curls, before Lucah's eyes settled on Dackon's, looking right through him.

For a moment, he could not breathe, before he retrieved his invisible knife, turned on his heel, and *ran*.

✽ ✽ ✽

Lucah did not know where he had ended up. He had never before been to this town: small, damp, and dark. A cradle for a corpse. But he quickly found a place to weep. An alleyway between a human-butcher and a smouldering wreckage, rife with the wails of the burning.

He slumped against the wall, covered his mouth with both palms, and *screamed* with everything he could. He screamed and he sobbed, tearing his lips with his teeth and his cheeks with his nails. He wept until he was visible, until passers-by fled, as if they could taste the blood and spittle on his tongue, mingling like an omen of death.

If Dackon left, Lucah would follow.

If Dackon abandoned The Crimson Dead, Lucah would set the ship ablaze with everyone aboard. He would watch them scream and wither and die, and he would ensure there were no survivors, if that was his captain's wish. No one would stand in their way.

But what if Dackon did not allow Lucah to follow? What if he was seduced, stolen, *slaughtered*? What if Lucah never saw him again?

Lucah would rather die.

He screamed, hitting his head with his fist, again and again and again, until he was dizzy, as if to knock sense back into his brain. He had to do something. He had to do *anything*.

He would not lose Dackon, not for anything in the world.

Lucah bit down on his fist, hard enough to draw blood. His own was never enough, but it helped, just a little, tasting the metal on his tongue. He could imagine it was Dackon's blood, though it was not quite right.

He knew not a thing about The Everdrowned. He knew not a thing about its golden-haired captain, except that the glimpse of her tan face made it clear she was of the Mundane.

Mundane.

Mundane, and therefore *killable*.

That was how it would end.

Lucah could kill anyone he wished to, whenever he wished to, but a human was almost too easy to slay, especially in contrast with the foes he had already slain. He had cut down more humans than he could count, and it had been years since he had last kept track.

With a shuddering breath, Lucah pulled out his fist, scraping his knuckles on his teeth. He forced his lungs to calm, though his heart still pounded in his throat, and he forced himself to stand properly, though he wobbled like with an infant's first step.

His face, bloodied and tear-stained and bruised, settled into something cold and cruelly calculating, especially as he imagined ripping that woman – that thief, that *seductress* – to shreds. Perhaps he would even do it with his bare hands.

Lucah was sure he could.

He scrubbed his face with his sleeve, swallowed the mouthful of tear-salt and blood, and he began to plan.

* * *

"Lu-Lu! Oh, oh, oh! You would not believe what I found when I—"

Lucah grabbed Ocellia by the shoulder, yanking her and her bubble in close. The fancy gold dagger tumbled from her hands, over the side of the ship, and plopped right into the water.

He positioned his mouth just beside the blood-clouded bubble, close enough that only she could hear the words hissed.

"We need to talk."

Lucah released her, and Ocellia blinked in bewilderment, before amusement overtook her features. She leant in, and her bubble pressed against his cheek: a startling chill. Lucah could suddenly feel the deck under his boots, the wind in his hair, the blood beneath his skin.

It was easier for him to think, for a moment, before his mind focused on the only thing of any importance.

His plan.

"What's wrong, Lu?" Ocellia whispered, spitting

bubbles at his ear and making him scowl. "Are you sad about Dackon again? Do you think he's fucked that pretty captain? Do you think she's got more to offer than you, hmm?"

With a violent glare, Lucah shoved her. "Underwater. Now."

Ocellia waggled her eyebrows, her water carrying her closer. "Are you trying to take revenge by fucking me, too? Because as flattered as I am, I'm going to have to—"

"*Now*."

Lucah grabbed her by the arm. He began to yank her back over to the side of the ship, but only made it two steps. Her water stretched, winding around his waist. In an instant, the two of them were tossed overboard, the water so chilly it made him wish to cry.

Ocellia's lips pressed against Lucah's, and he could finally breathe again. He gasped, the water cooling his lungs.

As lazy as could be, Ocellia stretched, unseeing of Lucah's peril, though it was written all over his face. But before he could speak, or figure out how to relay his plan, she turned back to him. With a shark-toothed grin, she grabbed him by the hand and tugged him away from the ship. The water rushed past them, as quick as a breeze.

The anchor became but a speck, and the pair came to a halt.

Ocellia twirled him around her, before leaning in with a grin. "I wonder what's got you so sad, Lu!

Have you given up already?"

Lucah did not waste a moment. "I'm going to kill that captain."

With the giggles of an innocent girl, Ocellia swam backwards, folding her arms behind her head. She relaxed as if slipping into slumber. Her eyes closed. "Of course. You're getting a little predictable, Lu." She raised a finger. "And I'm not helping."

His mouth fell open.

A moment of silence engulfed them, like the sea was swallowing them whole. Then, Ocellia cracked. She began to cackle once more, and Lucah found himself scowling.

"Kidding, kidding! Oh, of course I'm just kidding." She mimed wiping away tears. "You're too easy to fuck with, and too easy to fuck, too. You knew Dackon for, what, a day? Before you let him fuck you, I mean." Grinning, she rolled onto her front. "I like a good fuck, every now and again. But you're, you know, a desperate pet."

Lucah glared.

She giggled again. "Aren't you?"

He would have dropped to his knees the moment he and Dackon had first met. But he loathed to admit it. Lucah knew what his crew thought of him, and especially what *Ocellia* thought of him.

As though she could read his mind, Ocellia's face crinkled with merriment. "You're so funny! Oh, oh, oh, there's no one else quite like you, Lucah Shot."

She swam back to him. "How are we doing it?"

Lucah shifted. "Tonight. And it'll be with Dackon's sword."

"Ooh, how twisted!" Ocellia sighed. "You're so creative. I usually just go for the throat. I chomp right through, you know? I don't have the craftsmanship you do." She grinned once more. "You were made for this job, Lu. You know that, right? You're everything your god could have wished for! The perfect, pretty follower of Blood."

Though it was strangely textured whilst deep underwater, Lucah adjusted his waistcoat. "I know. That is why Dackon chose me."

Ocellia's lips twitched as if she disagreed.

For once, she did not voice it.

Lucah was not in the mood for that argument.

"You should have a victory fuck!" Ocellia chirped, so suddenly that it made Lucah recoil and blink. "You know, celebrate your victory over this bitch by letting Dackon fuck you one more time first, just so you're good and ready! And, you know, that'll get you Dackon's sword, too. You're shooting two targets with one arrow."

Her fists gripped the waves, her eyes aglow with vicious mirth. Had she ever looked anything but violent?

If she had, Lucah had not been present for it.

"That is not a bad idea... which is a surprise, coming from you."

"I know! Wait, was that an ins—"

"Take me back to the ship."

Ocellia pouted. "Already?"

"I want this done *quickly*, Ocellia."

With a heavy sigh, Ocellia waved dismissively. "Yes, yes. You're an easily-aroused man. The thought of murdering a rival gets you hard. I already knew that."

"She isn't a rival. He does not care about her."

"Well, we'll see, won't we?"

Ocellia shushed him before he could explain how little this captain meant to Dackon. She was nothing like Lucah, and Dackon loved and respected Lucah in equal measure, more than he could love and respect anybody else.

That was why Lucah was Dackon's first mate, and this woman was just someone he had known eons ago. That was why Lucah was at Dackon's side, keeping him young and beautiful forever.

And that was why Lucah was going to win.

No one would ever take Dackon from him.

Ocellia caught him by the wrist. They shot back in the direction of the ship, so quick that Lucah could not breathe, even whilst under the effects of her spell. With a leap, Ocellia and Lucah were out of the water, the latter tossed across the deck, whilst the former returned to the waves with something akin to a graceful ease.

As Lucah landed, sprawled like a starfish, many of their crew cackled: drunk and mocking. Lucah's face warmed, just slightly, but he truly did not care what they thought of him.

Dackon was the only one of importance.

Lucah adjusted his drenched clothes, wringing out his dripping braid, before taking it down entirely. He combed his fingers through his hair, his nails getting caught on webs and knots, before he spat a curse and let go. He needed an *actual* comb, and a way to dry himself, too.

He did not know when Dackon would return, but he would need to be quick if he wished to seduce him and take him to bed quickly.

What a delightful thing that would be, lovemaking only *hours* before killing the woman in his way. He would have much to tell her as he carved spiels of hatred into her flesh. She had to know the ways Dackon held and fucked Lucah: rough and quick and leaving marks with every touch. She had to know just how much Lucah *adored* him, and just how far he would go to keep himself in Dackon's bed.

She *would* know. That was the last thing she would ever know.

Lucah got to his feet, finally, and ignored the mocking calls that followed him wherever he went.

He needed better clothes. He needed not to look like a complete mess on one of the most important days of his life. Lucah was ridding Ungode of a monster, a vixen, a seductress: a bitch who could not keep her hands to herself. Anyone would thank him for that.

For a moment, Lucah clenched his jaw, before remoulding his face into serenity. He turned, marching over to the cabin door and finding it mercifully unlocked. He threw it open, and, in an instant, he knocked into a towering chest, almost falling onto his backside. But he was caught by the forearm just in time.

Before he could process what was going on, Lucah was dragged through the doorway, and the door was slammed shut behind him.

Lucah was pushed against it, a mouth sliding down his jaw and onto his throat. He melted into Dackon's touch, a groan slipping from desperate lips, especially as Dackon's hands slid under his shirt, under the undergarments below, and pressed cool fingertips against the bare flesh of his stomach. Then, Dackon grabbed him by the hips, grinding against him and inciting a high moan.

Everyone on deck could hear them; Lucah knew that. He had never been one to fuck quietly, and Dackon had no interest in hiding it. But Lucah did not care. He never had.

The only thing that mattered were the fangs against his throat and the fire in his veins and the hips pressed together, sending pangs of pleasure throughout him.

"*Please*," Lucah begged. "Please, please—"

Dackon needed nothing else. Sometimes he made Lucah beg, teased him for what bordered on *hours*, like he would never give in, like he could do this for eons. But today was not one of those days.

Lucah was filled with an immense relief.

He *needed* this. More than anything, he needed

this.

Lucah let Dackon touch him and kiss him, bite him and fuck him. He let Dackon do everything he wanted to, and he held not an ounce of regret, did nothing but whimper and whine. Blissful.

With a vigour unmatched, Dackon fucked like nothing else mattered, like that was his greatest skill, though his swordsmanship was even greater. Lucah savoured every moment with him as if it were his last, as if he would never be fucked again.

Dackon had been his first, but he could not imagine anything greater.

Well, perhaps sex after a gruesome murder – a victory in battle – *would* be something greater, something far unlike the pleasure Dackon had already given him.

And as Lucah pretended to drift into slumber, peeking through dark eyelashes, bare under thick blankets, Dackon dressed himself. He did not make a sound as he fixed his clothes and hair, did not wipe away the blood that stained his lips, and did not even look for his ruby-bejewelled sword. It seemed he did not need it.

Instead, Dackon simply left the cabin, leaving Lucah to release held breaths, now engulfed in a thick, empty silence.

Lucah sat up, combing his fingers through his mess of hair, and wiped away the blood that stained his bruised skin, both his and Dackon's ever-mingling in both of their hearts. He licked it from his fingers, pushed the blankets aside, and climbed out of bed.

There was a strange serenity that came when one dressed themself alone after sex, and especially so when the act had been so delightfully rough and bruising. Lucah did not regret it for one moment, even as his skin prickled with goosebumps, his heart longing.

He finished dressing himself quickly.

And, as soon as he was ready, he reached under the blankets, and took Dackon's hidden sword, speckled with ancient blood.

* * *

"How are you going to do it, Lu?"

Ocellia's bubble followed Lucah as he stalked through the streets, eyeing anyone who so much as glanced his way, and deliberately avoiding the paths of those who could have been pirates.

It did not matter if they were of The Crimson Dead or The Everdrowned. For now, both sets of crews were threats.

"With the sword," Lucah spat, ducking his head as he passed a woman with brown and gold locks, and dodging another with knives as black as her eyes. "Was that not obvious?"

Ocellia pouted, especially as he sped up. She matched him in an instant, before sliding into his path and cutting him off.

He glared.

"Lu-Lu," she said, shaking her head as if in

disapproval. "I did not ask what with, I asked *how*. There are many ways to kill! Are we torturing her, biting her in two, or slitting her throat and fleeing? And how many are we taking down with her?"

Lucah pushed past her. "Anyone we can."

Ocellia let out a high, cackling giggle, clapping her hands together with delight. "Oh! Oh! Oh! This shall be *so* much fun to watch!"

As Lucah's brow furrowed, his boot caught on a crack in the street, though he managed not to do more than stumble. He caught his balance, arms outstretched. "Watch?"

"Yes! That's what I said." Ocellia smiled. "Did you mishear?"

Lucah bristled. "No. But it's fine. I can do this myself."

"Can you?"

"Of course."

"Well, then what's the problem?" Ocellia's voice bordered on innocent. "You can handle it alone, and so I shall let you, then watch as you tear each other to bloody, bloody pieces!"

Ocellia's sugary words morphed into another cackle, her head tipping backwards. She followed as Lucah stalked down the streets, his fury only growing with every footfall.

Though Ocellia babbled on a little more, Lucah paid no attention.

The sea-salt scent grew stronger, leaving a taste of old blood on his tongue, as more and more pirates and sailors filled their path.

Lucah's arm ached at the weight of Dackon's sword. The hilt's gems dug into his skin. Its blade almost dragged along the ground. And yet Lucah could not bear the thought of sheathing it, lest he was unable to pull it out quick enough. What would happen if he failed?

He was going to kill her *slowly*. He knew that.

But he had to ensure she actually *would* die, even if she escaped after only one blow. Not that she would.

Lucah would slash her stomach open, letting her guts drip out. He would pierce every finger through the bone. Her eyes would squelch below his boots. And he would ensure her final moments were agonising. She would spend her last breaths begging for him to let her go, and he would *adore* it.

That was all she deserved, after all.

The pair turned a corner, and the docks were in sight.

Lucah's breaths fled from him. His head spun, his limbs wobbling, and he stumbled, falling against a brick wall and catching himself on the corner just before he hit the ground.

Ocellia almost did not notice, but floated back, whispering something merry that Lucah could not quite make out.

Why was he getting a bad feeling from this?

He had killed before. He would kill again.

And he was doing this for *Dackon*. This was no petty murder, no axe to the throat of an anonymous; this was something far better, something that had him salivating as he pictured fresh blood on this tongue.

And yet he was suddenly so afraid, unimaginably so.

"Lu?" Ocellia's words broke through his daze. She gave an awkward chuckle. "What's wrong? Don't tell me you're giving up!"

"I'm not," Lucah spat through gritted teeth. "I just—"

Fear.

This was no bad feeling.

This was not some mundane occurrence. He was not in the claws of natural panic, nor anything tinged by humanity. It must have been a blessed coin, though one worth more than any once held in his palm.

This was not *fear.* This was *Fear.*

Lucah's eyes widened, and he caught Ocellia's gaze just in time to watch the point of a silver blade protrude through her throat. Moments later, her eyes went wide, her mouth forming a circle. The blade was pulled back, and the bubble and Ocellia dropped as one, spraying reddish water from the wound and revealing a woman stood behind her.

She was tall, slim, bearing dark clothes and black braids, speckled with silver and blue. Her earring cast a shadow on her cheek. A coin, bubbling with Fear, slipped from her fingers and hit the ground, losing the remains of its blessing.

Lucah fell to his knees beside Ocellia before he

could process what was going on. He grabbed her arms, shaking her and coating his hands in the gushing crimson.

"Ocellia!" he cried. "Ocellia, let me—let me—"

He pressed both hands to her throat, slipping fingers into her wound, darkening his clothes with thick, sticky red. The blood made him wish to drink and sing, but the empty expression on Ocellia's face – eyes immovable, cheeks wet – made him wish to scream.

It reeked of poison, mingling with copper and salt, and he gagged between his desperate wails. Lucah dug his fingers into her throat, tearing skin and hitting bone and splattering blood.

Healing.

He had never healed before, not aboard The Crimson Dead. Dackon had forbade every attempt, had said it would only weaken the crew, that anyone who was killed had *deserved* it.

Lucah gagged again, hand flying to cover his mouth, but all that did was smear Ocellia's blood across his tongue and teeth.

She tasted of metal and salt.

He did not know how to heal her, though he poured every ounce of his magic into it. He did not know how to heal her, but even if he had, it was far too late.

She was gone.

Lucah's anguish was overwhelmed. He leapt to his feet, bloodied and screaming, and pounced at the woman who brandished the knife, fresh-pulled from his best friend's corpse.

She dodged with silent ease.

"I'm going to kill you!" he screamed. "I'll rip you to pieces! I'm going to make it *hurt*! You'll die and you'll die and you'll die!"

The woman ducked under his punch, raised a foot, and kicked him in the side. He fell to the ground, scraping the arm and leg he landed on, but leapt to his feet as soon as he could.

Agony echoed through every ounce of him.

"I'll tear out your eyes! I'll eat you alive! I'll—I'll kill you!"

"How, Lucah Shot? How are you going to do it?"

Lucah stumbled. How did she know his name? How did this *stranger* know his name? And what was so familiar about her face: cool, brown, and splattered with Ocellia's blood?

It struck him.

How had he been so foolish, not to expect this attack to be from—

"You're of The Everdrowned?"

The woman did not respond. She simply took a fighting stance, clutching the knife that had just killed Ocellia, and stared at Lucah as if nothing in all of Ungode would convince her to spill her secrets.

The Everdrowned was taking everything from him.

Lucah's heart stopped, before it felt as if it were being squeezed by a fist. He could not breathe, and then began to breathe so heavily it almost knocked him to the ground. It almost killed him.

Ocellia was *gone* and Lucah was going to follow.

He would never see Dackon again.

Lucah was going to die. He was certain of that.

His mind raced, his heart pounding and wailing, and salt dripped from his eyes, his vision tinged reddish from blood-splatters and rage. It only made him stronger, but it also made him scream. He was moments from collapsing, his breaths so fast he was lightheaded.

The other pirate simply tilted her head at him, looking him over with dark eyes that he suddenly registered were *utterly* mundane.

His fury overwhelmed him at once.

Lucah snarled like a ravenous beast, the blood on his skin seeping in and setting his nerves aflame. But he did not attack this woman.

Instead, he snatched Dackon's sword from the ground, turned on his heel, and *ran*. He would take a longer route – just to throw her off his trail, if she did choose to follow – but he was sure he would reach The Everdrowned before she did.

✳ ✳ ✳

Lucah hardly noticed he had lost his bag.

It had slipped from his shoulder, hitting the ground moments after Ocellia had, and one was far more notable than the other. He did not care. His bag, and its contents, were utterly, utterly irrelevant.

He still had the sword that left indents in his

palms. And that was what he cared for. He could no longer care about anything else.

The sword sang so sweetly to Lucah, splattered with Ocellia's salt-rotten blood – like his clothes, his flesh, his *tongue* – though this blade had never once scraped her skin. At least as far as he knew.

Dead. Dead. Dead.

Ocellia was *dead*.

He would never again hear that cackling laugh. He would never again see that smile. Even his memories of her, bubbly and bright, would remain ever-tinged by the new way he had seen her.

A dead-eyed corpse.

She would never breathe again.

Lucah breathed twice as hard, as if he were doing it for her.

He turned a corner, sprinting past a pair of women, hand-in-hand, and a bright-eyed toddler munching on a severed fist. He paid them as little attention as they deserved.

The salted stench returned, but he could hardly smell it over the blood that coated him. He could feel it sinking into his skin. He could feel it giving him energy. He could feel it empowering him, like it was some delectable treat, something to be savoured.

If it were not for the blood, he would not have been able to keep running, and certainly not at such a pace. But if there had been no blood, Ocellia would have still been alive.

She was gone.

Lucah knocked his head with his empty hand, veering left to dodge a crowd plucking flesh from a corpse for a feast. He caught sight of masts donned in gold, sails of a similar shade. The cackle of pirates reached his ringing ears, a violent song like no other.

Never before had he so wished he could not hear; never before had he so wished to be weak.

If he had never met Ocellia, he would never mourn her loss.

If he had never met Dackon—

Lucah slapped himself across the face, and then knocked his temple with the handle of Dackon's sword, all whilst he sprinted across the docks. He boarded The Everdrowned only moments later, and caught the attention of the crew in an instant.

Lucah swung before they could, and the head of a ginger woman slipped from her shoulders, hitting the deck with a thud, spraying blood like it was as plentiful as water.

A man with a quiver of arrows, slung over his shoulder, reached for his bow. A child with no business being aboard such a ship scurried below deck. A pair unsheathed their swords.

"All of you," Lucah muttered, dazed and dizzy, though he knew they heard him clearly. "I'm killing—I'm killing all of you."

He dodged an arrow shot his way, growing quicker with every splatter of blood, though he refused to pause to lick it from his fingers like jam from warm, wet bread.

An empty chair was thrown at his head and Dackon's sword split it in two. A dagger embedded itself in his arm, but he could barely feel it. Shouts carried across the deck, most people too in shock to do much more than watch. And Lucah cared not for any of it.

He inched closer to the captain's cabin, the hole already patched, the door remaining shut. Locked.

It seemed every pirate on The Everdrowned was more concerned with blocking the door than keeping Lucah from slaughtering them all.

He *would* slaughter them all. He was certain of that.

He would tear limbs from torsos, crunch bones beneath his boots, guzzle blood from weeping veins. He would *feast*.

Lucah would destroy The Everdrowned and destroy its captain and *destroy* the woman who had killed Ocellia. He would torment and torture and drink and vomit and cry. He knew that all with certainty. He knew his fate as if the words had been carved into his skin.

Lucah cut down another pirate, stomping on an axe aiming for his shin. He knocked over a scrawny man with his elbow, turning and raising his blade, readying it for plunging into the enemy's belly.

Just another human.

Just another corpse.

It had never, and would never, mean a thing.

His sword was wrenched from his grasp and Lucah screamed again, a predator wounded by prey. He turned, reaching for it as if he needed it to live. He did. He did. He did.

And he met the sharp, cold gaze of his best friend's killer.

She scowled, her painted lips curling in disgust.

Three pairs of hands caught Lucah from behind, binding his arms and holding him in place. He struggled, for a moment, before the enemy caught him by the chin. Her eyes were contemplative and cruel.

"Your captain means much to mine."

Lucah spat in her face. Blood. "Fuck you."

The woman raised an eyebrow. Her silver-streaked braids glinted in the sunset like little mirrors set aglow. Her nails dug into his face, but he refused to flinch. The blood on his skin was more than enough to keep him strong. He had never before been so powerful.

"Are you going to continue being difficult?" the woman finally asked, as Lucah struggled against the arms that bound him and the tips of blades pressed into his back.

"I'm going to kill you," he spat.

What else was he to do?

The woman raised her blade, still dark with Ocellia's blood. She pressed the point against Lucah's throat, before dragging it upwards: light and slow. Someone grabbed Lucah's braid, tilting his head back and exposing his scars in the manner reserved only for Dackon.

Lucah's belly curdled with fury, but he could not

move.

"Your captain means much to mine. And she doesn't particularly want me to kill you." She leant in, voice lowering to a whisper. "But I don't think she'd discipline me too harshly, if you were to… fall."

Her blade traced his lips, and Lucah exposed his teeth.

But the only movement he could manage was to run his tongue over his fangs. The woman's lips twitched in disgust.

"You've killed and maimed several of my people," she continued, her blade nicking the corner of his lips. "Your death would be quite justified. I don't know a soul who would disagree."

Lucah glared. "You killed Ocellia first."

"Where were the two of you journeying to?"

"That does not matter."

"See, I think it does."

The knife dug in: a spot between throat-scars.

Lucah caught a glimpse of himself in a different blade's reflection, watching as a bead of blood slipped from his skin, much alike a jewel dripping from a necklace, mingling with all that remained of Ocellia.

Lucah was certain he would throw up again.

At least they would be reunited. Somewhere.

His rage slipped, his chest aching with the need to fall. His eyes stung, and he went limp in the arms that held him, allowing his spider-lash eyelids to slip shut. At least he would die out of love.

Lucah did not listen to the commotion around him. Not until, all of a sudden, the knife was yanked back. He fell forward, hitting the deck with a thud. His hands did not catch him, but as his eyes flew open, fixing on the bloodied deck below, he began to push himself back up.

An instinct.

Lucah only lasted a moment before the kick collided with his ribcage. He groaned, head whacking against the deck, and rolled onto his back. He stared up at the now-towering woman, as those who surrounded her made no effort to intervene.

She flipped her dagger, spraying Lucah with even more of Ocellia's blood. It splattered across his shirt, dripping down his sleeves and staining any remaining patch of white.

The woman did not care.

Instead, she crouched, reached for the blade Lucah had forgotten was still embedded in his arm, and twisted it. He screamed, nerves on fire, and she yanked it back out, spraying fresh blood across the deck's existing splatters, all having yet to have dried.

Lucah could not move his hand.

Dackon would heal him.

His head snapped to look in the direction of the captain's cabin. The door remained closed, remained locked. Was Dackon inside? Was Dackon going to let him die?

Dackon would never do that to him. Lucah knew that.

The woman stepped on the wounded arm, her boot digging into the torn flesh, and Lucah wailed once more, like an animal, moments from being eaten alive. Those surrounding him only chuckled and tittered, entertained, more than anything else.

A tear dripped down Lucah's flushed cheek. He could not wipe it away, and he did not try to.

"Lucah Shot," came the voice of his tormenter. She paused. "Are you expecting to fight your way out?"

She stomped, and he bit right through his tongue.

"Fuck. You," he barely managed to spit.

The woman's boot landed back on the ground, and she tilted her head as she looked over Lucah as if he meant nothing at all, as if he were but a pest, as if he had not come to this ship to kill everyone aboard. As if he had not already begun to do so.

"Dackon doesn't keep his pets well-trained."

Lucah's eyes stung and body screamed. "Don't say his name."

What did she know? She was loyal to a traitorous bitch.

"Why not?" she asked. "You're not worthy of him, are you? Don't you know that?" She took a few steps forward until her boots were on either side of Lucah's hips. She leant down, blade dripping blood like a soaked rag. "You don't make for a very good pet."

"I've done everything I can to serve him."

"Have you? A good fuck, every once in a while, isn't worth the burden, I'd say. A captain of his status deserves better."

Lucah spat in her face, but she wiped the bloodied glob with her sleeve, utterly unbothered. What would it take to destroy her just as much as she was destroying him?

"Would this be doing him a favour?" she mused, tapping her knife against her leg. "He can find another follower of Blood to drink from. My captain can find a dozen more suited to our needs."

Lucah's fury returned like an arrow to the heart. With a strength almost unfamiliar, he raised his foot, and kicked her leg. She crumpled, falling on top of him, and he shoved her aside with the one arm that worked, leaping to his feet.

Dackon needed him. Dackon needed him. Dackon needed him.

There was a gap in the crowd – a glimmer of sunlight, peeking between rainclouds – and Lucah's eyes fixated on it. He pushed aside his anguish, his echoing pain, and *ran.*

The blood made him quick. He darted through the streets like a bird amongst breezes, like a dragon between mountains.

Forward. Left. Left. Right.

He skipped the street where Ocellia's body lay, his heart pounding to the rhythm of his footsteps. Lucah simply *ran.*

Blood gushed from several wounds,

strengthening and weakening him in equal measure, making him dizzy and delirious. He was going to vomit, like he had when he had first fled from her corpse. But he did not. He simply sprinted, half-stumbling – scraping bloodied knees against stones every mile or so – before the salted scent returned.

This time, though, it was even more nauseating.

Lucah slammed a hand over his mouth, gagging on bloodied bile.

He stumbled onto his ship.

A confused cacophony called after him as he fled to the captain's cabin, though none attempted to follow. He slammed the door behind himself, falling against it, before managing to make it to the bed.

It was covered in his and Dackon's blood – dried, mostly – and Lucah could not wait to bury his nose in the sheets. He fell into it, and, in his daze, hardly realised he had left Dackon's sword behind.

❋ ❋ ❋

The bed was too warm in Dackon's absence.

Dackon's hands were always so cool, so comforting, like a storm on a broiling day. His lips were almost equally so, except when stained with Lucah's burning blood.

Lucah had never feared his own blood before – not since he had been but an infant – but as it drained from his frail-growing body, he was suddenly so aware of how little power he held.

He could die.

He could, without a doubt, die. That was, if he remained alone.

Dackon would return soon.

Dackon would return soon, and he would hold and kiss and caress Lucah. He would talk to Lucah so softly, so kindly, in a tone he had never once heard in his beloved captain's voice. Lucah was sure it was there, though. He knew Dackon loved him.

Terror filled him to his core.

Lucah reached weakly across the bed, plucking a thick, stained pillow from his feet. He pressed his weeping face into the soft, flaky fabric, imagining the dry flecks of blood to be fresh from Dackon's pearly skin. Breathing made him cough.

How long did he have left?

Why had Dackon never taught him how to heal?

Lucah could think of nothing but Dackon.

That was what he told himself, at least, because he wished not to think about the other who occupied his mind. She swam amongst his thoughts as if undersea. Fishbones cracked against his skull.

Dead. Dead. Dead.

Ocellia was *dead*.

This was a nightmare. A dark, disgusting nightmare. There was no other explanation. He had tumbled into slumber, a deep sleep that only came from Dackon drinking from his throat too long.

He would awaken. Soon.

Lucah almost believed it. He had no other hope to hold on to.

Nothing. Nothing. Nothing.

Suddenly, the doorhandle rattled, and Lucah gasped, hand jerking and tossing the pillow to the floor. Was someone testing the lock?

It had to have been Dackon.

No one of The Crimson Dead would enter the captain's quarters. And no one not of The Crimson Dead could step foot on the ship, not without immediate slaughter. Lucah had heard no commotion, not even a *hint* of it. Still, something unsettled his burning stomach, even with his daze.

He raised his head, staring groggily as the door opened, revealing... nobody. Nobody, nobody, nobody at all.

Had it been the wind? That was impossible.

Lucah tried to sit up, but his head spun. His one movable arm gave out, and he collapsed onto the bed once more, sinking into the weak mattress. He was unable to do anything but watch as the door shut, and then locked, seemingly all by itself.

Invisible. Invisible. Invisible.

Lucah's mouth dried, but he would not have been able to speak, either way, as the dark-braided woman reappeared, slamming her hand over his bared teeth.

"Shh..."

Lucah could not have been able to scream, even had his mouth not been covered. There was little air in his lungs.

In the woman's hand was that familiar gold blade, embedded with rubies and covered with intricate engravings: prayers written to the god of Blood himself. Lucah and Dackon had always preferred human sacrifices as a means of worshipping their god, but it seemed the blade's blacksmith was of a different denomination.

It was strange that, in that moment, that was the thought at the forefront of Lucah's mind. And then it gave way to panic.

He struggled, but the woman's nails dug into his cheeks.

"*Quiet,*" she hissed, so forceful that he immediately obeyed.

Her legs landed on either side of his torso, and the point of Dackon's blade balanced in the centre of Lucah's chest, as if that was where it belonged. She pressed, light, and a pinprick of blood joined the rest that coated him entirely.

Lucah could not breathe, and most of that was not due to the hand that kept him from screaming.

"I wasn't going to do this," the woman whispered, her voice like stringed music, "but I'm sure you understand. We're both first mates. We're both pretty pets to the captains we worship, though only one of us truly understands what that means."

She leant in, her painted lips beside Lucah's ear.

"Do you know who you're worshipping? Do you know what they have done? My captain and yours are better than us in every sense. And I'm going to protect my mistress whether she approves or not."

There was a pause.

And then the woman tilted her head. "You wouldn't want to get in the way of that, would you?"

The blade pressed harder.

Lucah took a shaky breath, staring up with wide, wet eyes. For a moment, something strange flashed in the inky pools of the woman's gaze. Then, her eyes narrowed, turning harsh and cool.

"Don't forget," she hissed. "You'd do the same to me."

And Lucah would.

Had he been straddling her, with her captain's sword between his palms, he would not hesitate. He would kill her *slowly*.

Lucah's eyes darted to the door, and then back up at her. She did not cast even a single glance back over her shoulder.

Someone needed to come in. Someone needed to help him.

"Goodbye, Lucah Shot," came the whisper tinged with salt. "Die remembering the allies we could have become. Die remembering that you never truly had his love, did you?"

The sword rose. Lucah's breaths stuttered. And —

Drop.

The blade plunged into his belly, and Lucah wailed. It rose again, before plummeting with the violence of an avalanche.

Rise. Fall.

Rise. Fall.

Rise. Fall.

Lucah's blood kept him alive, but it would not keep him for long.

She left the sword in his belly, and finally let go. Lucah's head spun, his eyes painted with inescapable scarlet. He could not feel his legs anymore, and only one of his hands.

Just for good measure, the woman's fingers skimmed the hilt, twisting ever-so-slightly, before she slid from her spot on top of him, leaving the silver-gold sword in place. Her boots hit the floor with a thud, and Lucah almost breathed a sigh of relief.

It was *over*.

She leant in, and both her hands went to his lips.

One pried his mouth open, and the other reached in and grabbed the point of one knife-sharp tooth. Dazed, he could do nothing but whine as she twisted and *yanked,* pulling the fang right out.

Lucah choked on his blood.

She held the tooth between two fingers, looking it over as if it were some treasure, plucked from a chest. Then, finally, she looked back to Lucah. Their eyes locked.

For a moment, there was nothing, and then she

leant in again.

Lucah waited for an addition to the agony, for her next torture, but that was not what came. Instead, she reached out, placed a finger on each eyelid, and closed his eyes for him.

❖ ❖ ❖

Lucah drifted in and out consciousness.

He was kept alive by his blood, but as it drained, so did his life. His essence. His soul. He was going to die.

He was going to die. He was going to die. He was going to die.

Where was Dackon? Had he and that vixen sailed away? He would never do that to Lucah; there was no uncertainty there, not even a sliver. Lucah, despite everything, still had faith in the man he so adored.

But would Dackon return in time?

Lucah was going to die. His agony was already fading into a heavy paralysis. How many times had he gifted such torture to another? He had never expected it to feel like this.

He was going to die, and he could hear the merry cackles and cheers of his crew. He could smell the salt of the sea, mingling with the stench of his own blood. He could feel the bed beneath his crumbling body, where he had had the moments he treasured most.

Dying in Dackon's bed was its own strange

ISABELLE BISSON-ROUTHIER

torture.

Lucah could not open his eyes. He could not form any words on his tongue, his mouth full of bubbling blood. He could barely even *breathe*.

His heart ached more than the rest of him.

He hoped Dackon knew how much he loved him. He hoped Dackon mourned him until they were, one day, reunited. Somewhere.

There were gods, so there must have been an After.

Lucah would know soon.

The door creaked open, and Lucah inhaled sharply. For a moment, there was silence, and then there was a harsh breath, a slam of the door, and a rush of footsteps. A pair of icy hands grabbed Lucah by the shoulders, hands he could not mistake for anybody else's.

Dackon!

Dackon. Dackon. Dackon.

Lucah was dazed, dizzy, dying, but he managed to crack his eyes open, just a little, letting in beams of silver moonlight.

He caught a glimpse of Dackon's face of terror, and he melted into his arms, eyes fluttering closed once again. Was this a love returned?

"Who did this to you? Did she—did—"

Dackon's teeth clicked shut.

In the back of Lucah's silver-streaked mind, he wished desperately to beg Dackon to heal him, to drip his blood down Lucah's throat, to do something Lucah was *certain* Dackon could do.

He could not utter a word. He could not open his eyes.

Dackon said nothing.

And then he let go.

Lucah listened, cold and confused and so, so afraid, as Dackon crossed the room with slow, echoing steps, opened the door, and closed it behind him. The lock clicked.

Silence. Darkness. Pain.

And Lucah died alone.

ABOUT THE AUTHOR

Isabelle Bisson-Routhier

Isabelle Bisson-Routhier, she/her, is an author from the UK, who dabbles in fantasy most of all, and whose dream has always been to publish a book. This has, it seems, finally become a reality.

Many more tales are to come...

You can follow at @isabellebissonrouthier on Youtube, Tumblr, and TikTok.

Printed in Great Britain
by Amazon

41977738R00169